D0558927

The Granny Curse

and Other Ghosts and Legends from East Tennessee

Please return to:
ONEONTA PUBLIC LIBRARY
221 2nd Street S.
Oneonta, AL 35121
205-274-7641

ALSO BY RANDY RUSSELL AND JANET BARNETT

Mountain Ghost Stories and Curious Tales of Western North Carolina

The Granny Curse
and Other Ghosts and Legends from East Tennessee

By
RANDY RUSSELL AND JANET BARNETT

John F. Blair
Publisher
Winston-Salem, North Carolina

Copyright© 1999 by Randy Russell and Janet Barnett
All rights reserved under International
and Pan-American Copyright Conventions

DESIGN BY DEBRA LONG HAMPTON

Second Printing, 2002

*The paper in this book meets the guidelines
for permanence and durability
of the Committee on Production Guidelines
for Book Longevity of the Council on Library Resources.*

The front cover features a photograph of
Moody's old grocery store, which is a few miles
from the Gunning Cemetery.
Both locations play a role in "Milk and Candy."

Library of Congress Cataloging-in-Publication Data
Library of Congress Catalog Card Number: 99-046957

To
the staff of John F. Blair, Publisher

Contents

Introduction

WHEN ASKED if we believe in ghosts, we do not hesitate to answer.

Ghost stories are a part of the landscape in East Tennessee. Stories flourish in the mountain hollows the same as apple trees. Stories live in caves and behind waterfalls, upon and under the surface of the rivers. Stories are carved into the rock. Past lives take shallow breath in the worn-away names and dates on cemetery headstones a hundred and eighty years old. Lost names are carried on the wind. Lost names walk the roads.

The best way to know a place is to talk to the people who live there. A still deeper appreciation might be had by talking to the people who once lived there and are now gone; people who lived there fifty, a hundred, even two hundred years ago. What they have to say is in the folklore. It is in the stories they told, stories that are being told today.

Folklore cannot be separated from its setting. Nor can it be separated from the people, the folk, who created it.

When asked if we believe in ghosts, our feeling is that this question is like asking if we believe in people, in holding hands, whether we believe in mountains and waterfalls, in rain. Yes, of course we believe in ghosts. Ghosts are at least as true as roads.

There is no better way to touch the landscape than to discover the stories that live there. It is our fond hope that, like Letitia Edes Mountain, your appreciation and understanding of the mountains and rivers, and people of East Tennessee might grow a little each year.

Randy Russell and Janet Barnett

Acknowledgments

THE AUTHORS THANK ALL THOSE RESIDENTS of East Tennessee who patiently provided us with directions to site locations on our frequent visits. Especially helpful were the volunteers of the Sequatchie Valley Historical Association who allowed us entry to the Dunlap Coke Ovens Park museum when it was otherwise closed for cleaning.

Jennifer Laughlin, a published author and a ranger at Roan Mountain State Park, provided us with the precise location of the cemetery on Dark Hollow Road, while also informing us of a particular ghost's habit of jumping onto car bumpers at this location.

Donald Brookhart personally pointed the way to a written record of the petrified man of Grassy Cove, which was among the published works of Stella Mowbray Harvey available from the Chronicle Publishing Company of Crossville, Tennessee.

Katharine L. Trewhitt of Cleveland, Tennessee, patiently retold the details of the "Weeping Mausoleum" for our benefit. She also kindly provided us with a transcript of a talk her late husband, Frank Trewhitt, gave before the Tennessee Folklore Society in 1962. Without this assistance we would not have learned of the vampire corpse uncovered so long ago just a few miles east of Charleston.

Marty Silver, ranger and naturalist at Warriors' Path State Park, went above and beyond the call of duty in responding to our request for assistance when he cheerfully provided us with all the important locations for our story, "Candy and Milk," including the site of the grocery store owned and operated by Porter Moody. Marty is a specialist in local ghost stories and other folk tales associated with the area.

The authors also wish to acknowledge the friendship of Henry Wong and Carrie Gates, of the North Carolina Center for the Advancement of Teaching. We thank them both for their personal support in our effort to collect ghost stories and other interesting tales among the mountains that straddle North Carolina and Tennessee. We'd also like to thank Carolyn Sakowski, president of John F. Blair, Publisher, and author of *Touring the East Tennessee Backroads*, for giving us limitless access to her personal library of local history books.

Finally, we are pleased to acknowledge the friendship of Genelle Morain, professor emeritus at the University of Georgia. Her generosity of spirit is one that has helped us come to a better understanding of the world of spirits as they exist in folklore (only one of her academic specialties) and as they exist in real life. Thank you, Genelle.

The Granny Curse

and Other Ghosts and Legends from East Tennessee

Greasy Witches

Abigail and Agnes Dobbs knew ahead of time that the young man was coming to their mountain. The old sisters, who lived on Roan Mountain, discovered it using a method for seeing the future that is still in use today among those who have been taught the secret.

All that's required is a new candle, a mirror, and the right night of the year. At the stroke of midnight on Halloween, the eve of All Hallows Day, a lighted candle will reveal the future in a mirror's reflection. For this moment, and for a moment alone, an image of a person's future will appear hovering in the mirror just above one's left shoulder. If a girl is to marry, she'll see the face of her husband reflected there. Good things may be seen, and bad. A man who is about to be murdered will see his killer in the candlelit mirror.

It wasn't many weeks after Halloween, sometime in December, that a man named Riley found himself out of money, out of prospects, and fresh out of friends in early day Jonesborough. It was to his advantage to leave town, because he was in debt. At this period in the history of eastern Tennessee, the frontier community severely punished debtors who couldn't pay their bills.

Written history reveals to us that for major crimes, such as murder, robbery at gunpoint, and horse thievery, hanging was the usual sentence. Criminals so convicted were hanged at a particular location just outside of town. The penalty was so often decreed in the court at Jonesborough that a deep hollow that runs alongside the current highway on the north side of town was known for decades as Hangman's Hollow. An oldtimer in Jonesborough might be found today who still calls it that.

Although they weren't hanged, people found guilty of lesser crimes in the Jonesborough court didn't get off easily. Individuals were sentenced to be held in public stocks. Some had their ears nailed to the thick board that was locked around their heads. At the end of an hour or two, they would be set free. Well, most of the person would be set free. Sometimes the court ordered that one or both of a criminal's ears be severed and left nailed to the pillory as an example to others who might be tempted by crime.

Jonesborough also had a public whipping post. The court sentenced the number of lashes to be laid on and named the hour. Women were not spared from this punishment. Records reveal that a woman guilty of petty larceny was sentenced to receive ten lashes at the public whipping post one hot August day in 1788.

When a person ran out of money and couldn't pay his bills, Jonesborough wasn't the community in which he would prefer to loiter. Besides, young Riley was homesick. Unlucky in love, he'd come to the frontier to find his fortune and had somehow missed it. Before winter deepened, he set out to return home with no more than a heel of hard bread in his pocket. Home was the small family farm on the other side of the mountains in North Carolina.

Riley walked a long way. He found a barn to sleep in. He stuffed straw in his shoes to keep his feet warm and rubbed his hands along the soft belly of a bawling calf to thaw his fingers. Riley's route home was to climb the lower side of Roan Mountain and pass through the gap between the mountain and Sunset Rock. It was the same route used by patriots during the American Revolution. Those backwoodsmen were on their way to engage and defeat British troops in the famous Battle of Kings Mountain.

Climbing the gap, he was met by a cold, persistent breeze. It reddened his ears, and it seemed to slow him down a bit. Occasionally, he'd turn around and walk backwards to keep the wind off his face. Hoping to have made much better progress by nightfall, Riley found himself stranded as the sun set. The temperature dropped dramatically, and the young traveler thought he would be forced to crawl inside the twisted rhododendron thickets for what little shelter he might find there.

Just as he was weighing his options, Riley caught a whiff of smoke on the crisp night air. Wood smoke. He smelled it plain as day. Somewhere nearby a fire was burning. Riley hastened along the trail, peering left and right into the darkened landscape. Then he saw something. He rubbed his eyes with both hands to make sure it wasn't a ghost in the night. It was still there, a soft yellow light about the size of a pin, off in the distant woods.

He trotted toward it, tripping now and then, scraping his legs on the brush. The little light grew. It was the window light of a small cabin in an open clearing high on the mountain. A glow of warm light rose, too, from the chimney of the cabin. Riley broke into the clearing and was nearly stopped in his tracks by the wind. It hit him like a train.

Riley knew all about the wind on Roan Mountain. He'd been through the gap before, on his way to Jonesborough. But he didn't remember the wind being this strong or this cold. He barely believed a wind could be so strong unless it was a hurricane or a tornado. It froze the tears in his eyes and sealed shut the corners of his mouth.

Old-timers say that on certain nights, when conditions are just right, you can ride the wind on Roan Mountain. You can climb right on and fly. Riley had heard once of a Tennessee mountain burial that had to be postponed because the wind kept blowing the hole right along the ground until it was out of the cemetery.

There were large areas on Roan Mountain where the wind was so persistent no trees grew there. They called these treeless areas balds, and Riley found himself having to cross a bald to reach the cabin. Smoke rose from the chimney straight up, as if no wind at all blew on the other side of the treeless nightscape.

The cold wind continued to push with both hands against Riley's progress. When he breathed, it felt like ice came inside his body. With fingers frozen numb, Riley had to wipe frost from his face in order to see where he was going. If he didn't walk any faster across the bald, against the torrent of wind, he'd be frozen dead by morning. Already he couldn't move his eyes from left to right, but had to look straight ahead into the wind.

He ran as hard as he could and barely moved forward at all. By the time he flung himself onto the wooden steps to the cabin door, Riley's teeth were too cold to chatter without breaking. The door opened then, from the inside, and the wind stopped. Riley stumbled into warmth and the light.

"Thank you kindly," he said to two old women stooped in front of the fireplace.

Abigail and Agnes Dobbs welcomed the traveler into their home. They gave him hot squirrel soup in a large crockery bowl. It was made with strong spices and herbs. They fed him soft, warm bread with plenty of butter on top. Riley was so cold and so hungry, he barely talked at first. They took off his wet clothes and wrapped him in a blanket. Even after he was warm and comfortable, he barely talked at all. He was exhausted from his travels and his battle with the mountain wind and was about to fall asleep where he sat.

The old ladies asked Riley his name, and he managed to tell them that. They asked him if he was married, and he was able to say no. There was a joke he always said when church ladies asked him when he was getting married, and he repeated it to these two old ladies.

"I'll only be getting married if I have to, to get out of jail," he said. He meant to smile about it, and they were supposed to laugh. But later he couldn't remember if they had.

Riley was sure of one thing. These two ladies were too old and too ugly to marry anybody. That's why they lived alone on top of a mountain. Any relatives they might have, Riley decided, were probably too darn ugly to marry anyone, too.

Before he could tell the old ladies where he was from or where he was headed, Riley dozed off. He fell asleep between his words.

The two old sisters helped him into the loft built across one side of the cabin. Riley's clothes dried by the fireplace. He fell asleep wrapped in his blanket, thinking that Abigail and Agnes Dobbs were the most generous women he'd ever met, even if they were both as ugly as a mud fence patched up with tadpoles.

He slept on the loft floor. Riley dreamed this way and rolled that way, then dreamed that way and rolled this way until he woke himself up in the middle of a dream. Rolling over on his side to wrap himself back into his blanket, Riley caught light in his eyes. It came from between the floorboards. It was like someone had parted curtains on a full moon.

The old women stood in front of the fireplace. He could see them as plain as day once his eyes focused. They were both entirely naked. Their braids were undone. Long, flowing gray hair covered their shoulders entirely and reached nearly to the floor. They were laughing out loud at something, cackling actually, and they passed a lard can back and forth between them.

Riley stared through the gap between the floorboards. He tried not to blink. The sisters rubbed their wrinkled bodies with the lard from the can, coating themselves with it, every inch. They rubbed it on their legs, and elbows, and on their chins.

Riley thought their noses had grown twice as big as before. The old ladies looked like birds to him, their long gray hair like wings.

Abigail and Agnes Dobbs took up cloth sacks hung from pegs on the cabin wall. The old women said, in turn, a certain phrase, a rhyme, and up the chimney they flew. Riley was stunned. He didn't believe it. He threw off his blanket and came down the loft stairs in a bound. He couldn't find the women anywhere in the cabin, but he could hear them talking to each other.

Riley remembered the words they had spoken, and he said them out loud once or twice. He said them like a chant.

Willie Waddie, I have spoke.
Willie Waddie, remove this yoke
And let me rise like chimney smoke.

Nothing happened. The fire was stoked and would last for hours. They couldn't have gone up the chimney without being burned. The cabin door was locked from the inside. Riley paced the floor in front of the fireplace, thinking hard. He picked up the can of grease they'd used and coated his arms with it. He rubbed it on his legs, and elbows, and on his chin.

He stood on tiptoes and pointed his arms straight up. He spoke the words again. "Willie Waddie," he said. "Willie Waddie," he said again. "Willie Waddie, remove this yoke and let me rise like chimney smoke."

This time he lifted from the floor. And up the chimney he flew. Just like that.

He was up on the roof in a second flat, where he sat to catch his breath and look around. It was clear, and he wasn't cold. The grease kept him warm, he supposed. Riley could see the stars and the mountains off in the distance. The frosty treetops caught the starlight and seemed to flicker with patterns of tiny brilliances. Riley could see like he had the eyes of an owl. He watched the sisters, Abigail and Agnes Dobbs, fly off over the clearing, over the mountain bald, and across the face of the winter moon.

There was a rhyme they said before taking off.

> *Willie Waddie, I do cry.*
> *Willie Waddie, let me fly*
> *Like a blackbird through a cloudless sky.*

Riley recited the rhyme, standing on one foot. He followed them. He flew just like they did. It probably wasn't wise to fly around naked like that, day or night. Riley surely didn't know what he would say if anyone saw him, but he liked flying. He liked it just fine. They were moving faster than any horse could run. They flew as fast as a howl on the wind. Not much time at all went by before they came to a town. Riley recognized it. The buildings on the main street had stepped gables across the front of them. He was back in Jonesborough. It had taken him days to walk the same distance. About the time he realized where he was, the naked old ladies went down a chimneystack in front of him. Their gray hair looked like smoke going in.

When the women came back out, their sacks were no longer empty. Abigail and Agnes Dobbs had come shopping. They smiled at Riley and waved to him. They went directly to another brick chimney on another step-gabled building and slipped away from sight. He flew to where they were, and he went in.

Riley landed on the floor on his hands and knees. He bumped his elbow and his chin. He stood up and looked for the old ladies who'd come in ahead of him. He was in a storehouse, and Riley could see almost as well as if lamps had been lit, though no lamp had been.

Abigail and Agnes Dobbs filled their sacks with items from the shelves, from cases stacked against a rear wall. The old ladies called for Riley to come into the back room with them. When they spoke it sounded like chirping to him. He followed them into a room where barrels were stored.

They had opened the tap on one that held forty gallons of aged whiskey. There was a stack of new tin cups nearby. They each took one.

The grease must have made him thirsty. Perhaps it drew the fluids from his body. Riley had several sips. He forgot he was naked. The women cackled at him like chickens. He tried to figure out which of the old ladies was Abigail and which was Agnes. He wasn't able. It didn't matter really because one was as old and as ugly as the other.

They asked Riley how he felt about marriage again.

"I saw the face of my future husband over my shoulder in the mirror Halloween last," one of the women said to Riley. "And he looked just like you." She pointed her wrinkled, greasy finger at him.

"As clear as you're standing there now," her sister added. Riley swallowed the whiskey in his cup.

"It wasn't me you saw," he told the two of them. "I'm not marrying anyone, unless of course I was in jail, and it was the only way to get out."

Riley laughed to have told his joke again. And one of the women refilled his cup. The other brought a lump of sugar from her cloth bag and dropped it in his drink. That's when he saw his reflection in the cup, in the curve of the polished tin. Well, Riley saw *something* mirrored in the shiny metal. It wasn't the face of a man. It wasn't a man at all. Riley turned quickly around, but nothing was there. He drank his whiskey very quickly, then drank more.

Abigail and Agnes Dobbs told him it was time to go. Riley said he was coming any minute. He'd be right there sometime soon. But, they were in a hurry, and he was slow. The sisters left him there. They said their magic words and up the chimney they rose into the night.

Riley leaned from one side to the other when he walked. He couldn't think straight. Eventually, he decided to go. He remembered the words.

> *Willie Waddie, I have spoke.*
> *Willie Waddie, remove this yoke*
> *And let me rise like chimney smoke.*

He stood in the outer room and recited the lines time and time again. He stood on one foot and lifted the alternate hand high over his head and said the rhyme. Riley nearly fell. He switched feet he was standing on and tried it again. Nothing happened.

The words wouldn't work for him. He rubbed his hands along his arms, feeling the grease that coated him. He rubbed his chin. It felt silky. It felt like feathers or fur.

So did his tongue. Riley tried again and again, but he couldn't say the words right. His mouth was dry.

He hurried to the back room. He turned the handle on the barrel tap. The distilled liquor poured onto the floor. Rather than find his cup, or get another one, Riley dropped to his hands and knees and licked at the growing puddle of whiskey. Once he'd had his fill, he stood up to go back into the outer room and stand next to the chimneystack.

Nearly too drunk to walk, Riley stumbled into the larger room. He stood on tiptoes and pointed his arms straight up. Then he tried to stand on one foot and hop just a little to get started. Muttering drunken gibberish, he lost his footing and fell forward between two rows of shelves, where his mumbles soon turned to snores. It was where he was found, completely naked and fast asleep, when the shopkeeper came in later that morning to open his store. They had to wake up Riley to arrest him.

The judge listened to his story. Riley told him every word. Riley told him all about Willie Waddie. He told the judge about witches and about flying on the wind. The sheriff of Washington County, who'd brought Riley to the court in chains, tried not to laugh at the sorry young man's incredible story. The judge didn't believe him either.

A barrel of whiskey cost more than Riley could afford. It was clear to the judge that the young man wouldn't return to pay his debt once set free. There were other small debts, it was revealed to the court, that the young man owed in town. The judge sentenced Riley to be punished and decreed a writ that the shopkeeper was allowed to charge twice as much for hard drink for the next six months or until he'd made up the cost of the lost barrel of whiskey. Courts strictly controlled the prices of nearly all goods in the frontier towns of eastern Tennessee.

Riley was sentenced to be held in the pillory for one hour, his ears nailed, and both ears then removed. A barrel of whiskey cost more than two ears' worth, however. The judge also sentenced Riley to be branded with the letter *T* on the cheek or forehead, so that all might know him as a thief and be warned. As a matter of routine, Riley would be banned from Washington County for the duration of his natural life.

The sentence was to be carried out the next day. At this time in the history of Jonesborough, it was quite uncommon for miscreants to be held in jail for long. Jail time was almost never itself a sentenced punishment. This was because the jail was the back room of a log house behind the courthouse. When anyone was being held there, the sheriff had to spend the night away from home or pay from his own funds for someone else to watch the prisoner.

Riley was given a cold supper of cooked corn and beans. His left boot was removed and a leg iron, attached to a length of chain, was locked around his ankle. The other end of the chain was fastened to a circle of iron hammered into the middle log of the exterior wall.

The sheriff, his rifle nearby, bedded down on a cot in the front room of the old log house. The fireplace was lit. He had little trouble falling asleep. Once a burning log shifted in the fireplace, and the sheriff came awake briefly. A little later, he woke again. He heard voices. Female voices.

Perhaps they were ladies from the church come to pray for and convert the prisoner. But that usually happened when there was to be a hanging. The sheriff listened hard. It sounded like women chanting or saying prayers in the back room. But how had they come inside? If the womenfolk had come in while he was sleeping someone would have had to unlock the front door and it was barred from the inside. The sheriff was the only person who could have opened the door. Unless the prisoner had broken his chain.

At this thought, the sheriff jumped to his feet, knocking his cot over sideways in a clatter. He rushed into the back room. He couldn't see well at first, but there was a little light coming in through the high window. The sheriff thought he saw the prisoner, all shiny like he was wearing a coat of wet paint, stand up from the floor.

He thought he saw Riley keep on standing up, getting taller and taller, and taller yet, until it seemed like the prisoner was flying straight up, lifting from the floor altogether, like a column of smoke rises from a campfire. There was a distinct movement of shadows nearby and the female voices were clearer now, though the sheriff still didn't know what they were saying. Something about a yoke.

As the stunned lawman of Washington County watched in disbelief, Riley flew out the little window, leaving his locked leg-chain on the floor.

The sheriff lunged for him. But it was too late. Riley was gone into thin air.

The sheriff wasn't slow to find his way out the front door of the log house. His rifle in hand, he circled the jail. Not even a dog was anywhere near. A moon shadow moved upon the side of the building, and the sheriff looked up to see a bushel of twinkling stars in the cloudless winter sky. If he saw anything that look like witches, the sheriff never said. Nor would he.

There was a greasy footprint on the jail floor—the only thing Riley left behind. It was the imprint of a foot as plain as day, a foot with five round toes.

No one figured out exactly what the grease was made of. No matter what they used for soap, the footprint would never wash away entirely. The log house burned to the ground in the 1820s, or the footprint might still be visible today.

Soon after Riley escaped, some of the shop owners put heavy screens over their chimneys. Still today, when the wind blows down from Roan Mountain late at night people in nearby towns, and in a few towns far away, are likely to find things missing from their stores. And when the wind blows down from Roan Mountain in the middle of the afternoon, Tennessee folks often say they can hear the faint and distant sounds of church bells upon the wind.

There is a little church up Roan Mountain way. And there is a church bell they ring, at times when there's a wedding and such.

Ghost in the Fireplace

We all see something different when we look into the dancing flames and smoldering coals of a wood fire. Scenes from the future flicker there, scenes from the past. A current daydream rises with the smoke. Our deepest loves are seen while gazing into a burning fire.

And so might be our fears. The crackle and pop of burning wood, it is said, is Satan snapping his fingers. It is known throughout the mountains that a fire, any fire, has one foot in hell and the other ready to burn down the house.

Something hoof-footed, and more shocking than lightning and thunder, has been known to emerge from the flames of a cozy log fire of an East Tennessee evening. In Unicoi County, a large, stampeding ghost rises from the fireplace, while wood is burning. It races about the room, crashing into things and causing a frightening commotion before it disappears back into the fire and up the chimney.

It's not the ghost of a man that comes raging out of the fireplace, but that of a horse. People who have experienced the clamorous terror of the oncoming ghost say that after it leaves by the chimney, the pale horse can be heard walking around on the roof. Eventually, it leaps to the ground and races away on resounding hooves.

The horse belonged to Holland Higgins, an Irishman, who home-steaded an area of Unicoi County marked by a branch of water that has since been named Higgins Creek. Holland was killed by a fiery-tempered hermit named David Greer, who was in the area at the time to herd cattle as a paid laborer.

David Greer, also known as Hog Greer because his living habits were said to be similar to that of swine, was famous for living in total seclusion on Big Bald Mountain and for having a violent temper. Big Bald Mountain is still called Greer Mountain by some. Greer made his nest in a sort of a cave on the side of the mountain and, curiously, encircled his home with a dry moat.

In his book, *Greasy Cove in Unicoi County*, Pat Alderman documents some of Hog Greer's life. Greer built a log cabin over a spring near the north fork of Higgins Creek. He left a floor plank loose and, by lifting it, could dip fresh water from the spring without having to leave his home.

Holland Higgins rode Cloud, his favored horse, daily around Unicoi County. Cloud was a tall, spirited stallion that seemed to read Holland's mind in the saddle. When Holland thought *left*, Cloud moved left. When Holland thought *go slow*, the horse did. Cloud was a white horse, but not perfectly so. There must have been a bit of roan mixed in with the pat-tern of his coat. To most, he looked to be the color of ashes. His mane and tail were darker than the rest of him.

Hog Greer wanted that horse. He offered to trade a small cache of mined silver for him.

Holland wasn't interested. He said that Cloud was the most loyal friend he had in this world and that he would be as likely to sell one of his sons.

It was the end of November when Hog Greer murdered Holland for his horse. That's what everyone thought was the reason. Of course, no one but the horse saw it when the hermit knocked Holland out of the saddle with the stock of an old mountain gun. The horse reared on its hind legs, kicking the air with his front hooves at the height of a man's head.

The hermit ducked the horse and fired his rifle into the chest of Hol-land Higgins, where the homesteader lay on the hard ground. At the sound of the rifle shot, Cloud bolted. Although Hog Greer had meant to grab hold of him, the horse dashed away. Greer turned his back on his victim and walked away.

Cloud showed up riderless at the Higgins house. He then led one of Holland's sons to the body. The boy draped the body of his father over the horse, and Cloud gave Holland his last ride home. Once the body was moved indoors, Cloud refused to be ridden. By anybody. He stood on his hind legs when approached. He bared his teeth and snapped at everyone.

Interestingly, the horse did something else. He paced.

He rocked back and forth in the little stables Holland had built for him. He wouldn't eat a bite. He stepped from side to side. Finally, Cloud broke out of the stall in the middle of the night and headed down the road at a full trot.

Holland was laid out for his wake on the day Cloud arrived in the dead of night at Hog Greer's cabin. The big, white horse kicked in the front door of the cabin and, with his head ducked, raced into the house. The hermit was scared, too scared to move at first, but he quickly got hold of his rifle and fired on the horse. He missed.

The stallion charged the post that held up the loft where Greer had been sleeping. He literally knocked the man out of bed and rolled the hermit off the overhead planking. When Greer fell to the cabin floor, he was soundly kicked. He ended up next to the fireplace, where he grabbed a burning log in both hands, searing his own flesh. He then swung the log directly at the horse in a wild, arching motion.

The cascade of burning embers and flames startled Cloud, so Greer was able to get away that night. He rinsed his blistered hands in the cold water of North Higgins Creek. People say Greer left that very night, afraid that the enraged horse of the man he'd killed would find him. Hog Greer took his gun and abandoned his cabin built over the bubbling spring. He headed back to Big Bald Mountain, where winter had already settled in.

Meanwhile, upstanding men of the neighboring farms formed a group to round up those in the area who might be capable of committing the brutal murder. These suspects were invited to view the body of Holland Higgins. They did so willingly. Each, in turn, was asked to touch the corpse. Each did.

In those early years, it was believed that the corpse of a victim would bleed when touched by the murderer. Some believe this yet today. Even those who were not suspected of doing evil touched the body, to show they were at peace with the deceased. The body bled for no one.

But no one could locate Hog Greer. His cabin was a mess. The door was loose. The coals had gone cold in the fireplace. Greer didn't come to the funeral and wasn't available for touch testing. He was noticeably absent.

When Holland was put into the ground, it was a cold day in early December. At the funeral, two of the mourners remarked that they had seen Cloud walking slowly on the road that ran along the Higgins homestead.

"He's been doing that ever since the murder," Holland Jr. said. "There's no sense to it. He walks up the road a few miles then turns around and walks back. Just misses the old man something awful, I guess."

For weeks after the funeral, Cloud walked to Hog Greer's abandoned cabin to see if the hermit had come back. Once there, Cloud would kick in the front door. Although the door was nailed shut time and again by neighbors, Cloud would return and kick it in. Each time, the aging stallion walked into the cabin, snorted a bit, turned around, and walked directly out. Cloud would then walk back to the road, back to the Holland Higgins homestead.

The horse wouldn't stop.

Everyone who lived along the little road saw Cloud trod slowly by. He walked by the church on Sunday morning and again on Sunday nights. People offered the horse food now and then. Holland Jr. even hung a bucket of oats every morning on the fence post out front, but Cloud walked right by it. There were some pretty fat squirrels in the yard that December.

Women brought red apples out and set them in the road as Cloud approached. The weakening white horse walked on by.

"Won't eat a bite of anything," Holland Jr. said. "I'm afraid Dad's old baby will be dead before winter's over."

One day, a neighbor told Holland Jr., "We have news. Me and two more, we found Hog Greer. He's back up to his place on Big Bald, that old cave. He lives on his belly back in there under those rocks."

"Maybe he didn't do it," Holland Jr. said. "Maybe someone else did."

"There's nobody else," the neighbor argued.

Holland Jr. pointed out that there had been some threats made against his father when the family lived near Embreeville, before they moved to the homestead now occupied by their family. Maybe those threats didn't mean a thing, but he couldn't be all the way certain yet that Hog Greer had shot his dad.

"But that's not all the news," the neighbor went on. "Well, old Hog won't let anybody come near at all. He shouts at you and then takes to firing that old gun he's got."

"Sounds the same as always," Holland Jr. said.

"Here's what's not the same, Holland. The crazy coot has dug himself a big ol' ditch. He's still working on it, I 'spect. Already it's four feet wide and deeper yet. We hollered at him what he was digging that moat for, and he said it was to keep animals out."

"Wild animals are up there, that's true," Holland said, shaking his head back and forth.

"It would trip a bear, I imagine. Well, you could get right in there and have yourself a sit-down picnic without your head ever sticking out, Holland. And, you know, it was more than wide enough a horse couldn't jump across."

Despite the news of Hog Greer's strange behavior, Holland Jr. still remained uncertain that Hog was his father's murderer. Meanwhile, Cloud continued his own strange behavior. Holland Jr. thought he might put Cloud out of his misery, but he couldn't bring himself to kill his father's favorite horse. He remembered his dad describing Cloud as a friend. You can't just shoot your father's friend because he's in mourning, no matter how unhealthy he becomes.

Every morning Holland's son set out a bucket of well water for Cloud. Every morning he'd break the ice out for the horse. If Cloud was drinking any, it wasn't very much.

Some of neighbors said the horse wasn't grieving—that Cloud was, instead, looking for revenge. They pointed out that the old stallion knew who the murderer was. They believed the horse was waiting for the killer to come back. They believed the big, white horse would chase down the murderer the minute he saw the man, chase him down and stamp Hog Greer to bits if he ever showed his face on that road or returned to his old cabin again.

Some of the more romantically inclined neighbors said the horse missed his master and faithfully waited his return. They thought they saw Cloud stopping each day at the little graveyard by the church before moving on.

Either way, Cloud trod on day and night, his head dropping lower and lower. His white tail and belly were coated with dirt, his mane badly matted. No one could keep the horse from his appointed rounds. No one could catch him when they cared to try.

Then one day before Christmas, Cloud quit. He simply sat down and died.

That spring, funny things happened. People kept hearing Cloud walking on that road at night. There was nothing there at times. Other times, people would swear they saw Cloud. They said the white horse would ride up to them and then pass right on by, without noticing anything but its own progress. You'd have to believe in ghosts to believe that happened. Yet, people said it did. People still do.

Greer's old cabin was patched up. New people moved in. Holland Higgins's son won claim to large tracts of land, including the little homestead they lived on. They owned Greer's old cabin, but they let other folks live there. No one lived there long.

The people who tried to make the place their home said the front door kept blowing open. And when they finally got the door where it would stay shut—and that was with some doing—then the fireplace acted up. A strong wind would blow down the chimney, and the noise sounded just like a horse was in the house. The wind was so strong it blew over furniture that wasn't nailed down, but it never blew the fire out.

It was about then, the locals think, that Cloud got mixed up. Or maybe he was just more determined to find that rascally hermit, Hog Greer. The same strange things started happening to other houses. People said they heard a horse walking on the roof, then it would come in and out the front door. Once in awhile, that horse would come out of the fireplace, dash about, and then head back up the chimney. It must have been an unsettling experience when the big, white horse came roaring from the flames and ashes to race through the house, hooves pounding upon the wooden floor, only to disappear up the chimney. People who knew the circumstances, knew the phantom was Cloud. They'd tell the horse not to come back, and he wouldn't. Not for a few years, anyway.

In some parts of the country, people hang a horseshoe over the door for good luck. Some people who own homes and resort cabins on both sides of the state line in the vicinity of Big Bald Mountain have been known to hang a horseshoe in the fireplace for the same reason. Still others in the East Tennessee mountains keep a horseshoe in the fire itself. It's supposed to bring good luck—and keep the ghosts at bay.

Visitors to the area who find a horseshoe in the fireplace should know if they remove it they are doing so at their own peril. Cloud is far from ready to abandon his search. Some may see the widening eye of a stallion where others see a burning ember.

The area where Hog Greer had his cave-like dwelling place on Big Bald Mountain is easily found today. It's been photographed time and again. There are also pictures of the remains of the big ditch he dug to protect his hermitage from animals, if you can't get up there to see it for yourself. The moat has filled in some over the past 160 or so years.

Pat Alderman records in his book that a grave marker, located near Temple Hill School in Unicoi County, reads:

> *Holland Higgins Sr.*
> shot and killed by David Greer
> *Nov. 30, 1824*

It was a long, long time ago. Maybe horses are like elephants when it comes to injustice—they never forget. Although he appears to have escaped the relentless pursuit of Holland's white stallion, Greer was shot to death in a dispute with a blacksmith name George Tompkins in the spring of 1834. No one knows the location of his grave, but you can bet it doesn't have a fireplace.

Dakwa Ka-Plunk

"Let me tell you a story," John Brown said to his guests at the tavern he owned and managed on the Moccasin Bend of the Tennessee River. Brown, a Cherokee, also operated the ferry here. This important crossing was a vital link in the old Federal Road, the only passageway between the deep South and eastern markets.

John Brown's tavern was erected in 1803 by Casper Vaught, who had been sent to the area by Colonel R.J. Meigs, the federal Indian agent to the Cherokee. The tavern was a two-story log home with a dogtrot walkway down the center, front to back. A front porch extended across the entire lower floor. The inn's two stone chimneys at either end of the house, each more than eight feet wide, were impressive. Guests were confident when spending a warm night and morning at John Brown's tavern.

And there were many guests. Just as there were many travelers, families, and traders, who used the ferry to cross the Tennessee River at Moccasin Bend, where the river snakes along the base of Lookout Mountain. By all accounts, John Brown made a killing. But he had a way to take in more profit than the usual innkeeper did during the early years of American expansion.

Being a Cherokee, Brown possessed a wealth of stories, the telling of which surely enthralled his guests who were traveling at the edge of wilderness.

Brown was also of a friendly disposition. His company was enjoyed by most of those who used his ferry and stayed at his inn. After dinner, he told weary travelers spirited Cherokee legends of a witch with an elongated spear-like finger for plucking out a child's liver, of underground panthers, of a slant-eyed giant named Tsulkala.

Known for his generosity, Brown would give away small amounts of tobacco and handcrafted smoking pipes to men who stayed at his inn, just so they might step out on the porch at night and enjoy a smoke with him. At times he would even entice some of them to walk to the river's edge with him, where he would check on the ferry before going to bed, and say a few words in Cherokee to the young boy who slept at the site. The youth's mission was to raise alarm should anyone or anything threaten the safety of the travelers' wagons and horses.

When inviting a guest to walk down to the river, Brown would say, "Come to the water with me, and let me tell you a Tanasi story." Tanasi is the Cherokee word for the big river that was changed to *Tennessee* when pronounced by white pioneers and settlers in the area.

It was at the river's edge, or while crossing on the ferry, that Brown told his best stories. These were the Cherokee water stories—detailed accounts of water cannibals, a haunted whirlpool, and a monstrously oversized leech. Of course, there were also stories about fish.

John Brown would often take travelers and their supplies across the river at night, or in the pre-dawn hours of the morning. This was especially important when a trader wanted an early start on dry land before the July or August sun rose and began to slowly cook the southern border of Tennessee into a sweltering heat.

A river doesn't sleep quietly at night, if at all. It churns and eddies. Fish jump. Mud hens squawk. Bear, deer, bobcats, raccoons, opossum come to the river at night. Logs jam other logs and brush. And every once in awhile something goes *ka-plunk*.

On many a night, John Brown would tell his guests his favorite Tanasi tale—the story of Dakwa.

Dakwa was a giant fish that lived in the Tennessee River. The giant fish could easily swallow a man. To demonstrate the size of Dakwa's mouth, John Brown held his arms in a large circle, fingertips touching fingertips.

He would then say that Dakwa's mouth was twice as big as this circle.

"Dakwa has barbs at both sides of his mouth, like a catfish," Brown said, as if the fish lived in the river still. "The barbs are scarlet. All man-killers have red at their mouths."

Brown went on to tell of a Cherokee warrior who was crossing the river in a canoe. The hungry Dakwa rose up under the boat with such force it flipped the surprised warrior high into the air. When the warrior came down, Dakwa was waiting at the surface of the water with his huge mouth open. The warrior fell in.

"Right over there at that spot," John Brown said, pointing. Cherokees always knew the exact location of their stories.

Brown continued his story. He said that Dakwa snapped its mouth closed and dived to the bottom of the river. The fish rested there, its belly full. The warrior regained his senses while sitting inside Dakwa. The young man was uninjured, but he was afraid he would suffocate be-cause there was so little air inside the fish. A fish can breathe air from water. A man cannot.

The warrior felt around in the darkness for his spear. It wasn't with him. Neither was his knife. What he found were stacks of mussel shells the fish had swallowed over the years. He broke one open and used the broken edge as a knife to cut his way out of Dakwa's belly.

It irritated the giant fish to have his stomach scraped with a mussel shell. He swam to the surface of the river and thrashed the water with his tail until the whole river was covered with foam.

The warrior continued to scrape at Dakwa's stomach until he got a hole started.

Water poured in. The warrior worked frantically until he managed to open a hole in the side of the giant fish large enough to slip through. Finally, the warrior swam free.

Dakwa was not killed, but was very embarrassed to have a hole in his stomach. He was so humiliated that he never came to the surface of the river again. Brown warned that Dakwa still sat on the bottom of the river, his side closed up with mud.

The warrior found that he was changed by the experience. Others in the Cherokee town noticed it when he came home. The acidic slime of the great fish's stomach had scalded the hair from his head, and he was bald ever after.

That was the end of John Brown's tale.

At this point Brown would punctuate the end of the story by dropping into the water a heavy stone from a pile of native rocks that he kept at one end of the ferry. *Ka-plunk.* He'd lift the rock over his head when no one was watching. *Ka-plunk.* It was an effective sound effect, which brought a startling end to his story.

But sometimes he didn't drop the rock into the river. Instead he brought it down swiftly, and with direct aim, upon the head of the unsuspecting ferry customer. It's a true story. The amiable Cherokee innkeeper was a serial murderer.

His motive was robbery. It paid better than putting a plate of biscuits and gravy on the table of a morning for travelers who spent the night in the log house. It paid more than the nominal fee he charged to ferry wagons, horses, people, and their dogs across the Tennessee River at Moccasin Bend.

The fee to cross the river on John Brown's ferry at night was sometimes blood. More than one traveler paid with his life. If John Brown was lucky, his victim paid with a fine gold watch and chain, a leather purse of current coins in silver and gold, a gun, a knife, pots and pans. Brown took whatever he wanted from the customer's wagon—including human lives.

It wasn't what was in the Tennessee River that proved dangerous to ferry passengers. Dakwa did not rise from the rolling water to swallow them whole. It was the man who lived on the river who proved to be the real risk to travelers at the edge of the American frontier. John Brown must have chosen his victims wisely and with care. His murders weren't discovered in his lifetime. Perhaps he killed only lone travelers. Perhaps he limited his robbery and murder to traders on the old Federal Road.

Once John Brown killed and robbed his victim under the cover of darkness, he weighted the body with rocks and threw it into the river. Ka-plunk. Then he rolled the traveler's wagon off the edge of the ferry into the dark, moving water.

Perhaps one or two of his victims had only been knocked unconscious by the murderer. Perhaps, badly injured and weighted with heavy stones, they saw the river flow over them as their life slipped away. Maybe they saw the giant Dakwa sitting on the bottom of the river nearby.

The identities of his victims are unknown. They were not unfound, however. Fifty years later, long after the Indian removal of the 1830s was history, dredging operations in the location of John Brown's ferry uncovered a line of broken wagon parts. It followed the course of the ferry crossing, from one side of the river to the other.

Discovered among the decomposing wagon pieces were human bones. The bones were embedded in the muck, in a line across the river like beads on a necklace, precisely in line with John Brown's ferry crossing. John Brown concluded his life on this earth without ever being brought to justice for his crimes. Some chroniclers of the past say he was forced west during the final Indian Removal, one of the few men of wealth to traverse the Trail of Tears.

Today when weather conditions allow, you can see the location of John Brown's ferry crossing at Moccasin Bend from Lookout Mountain. Sometimes from that lofty perch you can see something big move just under the surface of water. At another spot is a whirlpool that might be the result of Dakwa moving his tail at the bottom of the Tennessee River. You can't see all the way to the bottom, of course, no matter how high you get.

There is a way, however, to see under the river. And you don't have to be hit in the head and weighted down with rocks to do it. Visitors to the Tennessee Aquarium in Chattanooga can see what the bottom of the river looks like. Among worldwide exhibits, the $45 million aquarium replicates the habitat, fish included, of the state's major bodies of water. You can see the bottom of its lakes and both the Mississippi and Tennessee Rivers.

More importantly, visitors to the Tennessee Aquarium can expect to emerge from the exhibits fully alive and with at least as much hair on their skulls as they had when they went in.

The Cussing Cover

*E*verybody said Basil Estep's first wife killed him. And everybody in Cades Cove knew why. It was because he put her quilts on a metal bed and jumped in under them with another woman.

Mavis lived in a two-room cabin on Whistling Branch, behind Peter Cable's place in Cades Cove. She lived in that little valley surrounded by mountains all her life.

She was born during a thunderstorm. Her mother was called to straw when the storm first started down Gregory Bald Mountain. Mavis made her first scream while thunder clapped at the top of the trees and shook all the shingles on the house. It rained like cats and dogs fighting for two straight days after.

A baby born during a thunderstorm was fated to be struck by lightning. Mavis knew it. Her momma knew it. Mavis was never allowed to stay outdoors once the clouds rolled together. Anytime it felt like it might rain, she came immediately inside. Mavis never slept in a metal bed.

Most people in Cades Cove worried about being run up on by a mountain panther or a black bear. Some were afraid of rattlesnakes or of being bitten by dogs.

Mavis feared thunder and lightning.

She married Basil Estep. Her older brothers built a cabin for her. Mavis wouldn't let a metal bed into the house. She never slept on one. Neither did Basil. There was no metal on their bed anywhere. There were no metal springs, nor a metal frame of any kind. Mavis didn't want to be struck dead by lightning in her sleep.

Basil didn't mind it. They had a good mattress and on top of that was a big square of fine feather tick. With soft pillows and warm covers, you didn't know better sleeping than this.

Mavis was careful about things too. Once it thundered, or the outdoors got that water-on-dust smell that it has just before a rain, you couldn't make her take hold of a ladle. She wouldn't touch a pot handle, or even so much as a needle. Once it thundered, Mavis took the pins out of her hair and let it fall loose over her shoulders.

Needle and thimble were the hardest parts for her to set aside when it rained. Mavis loved to sew, and she was especially talented at it. She made the finest patchwork quilts and could do any pattern from having only seen it. Mavis was prideful of her quilting and made fine examples of Log Cabin, Tulip, and Lovers Knot. She had Snake Fence, Mill Wheel, Snowdrops, and Indian Hatchet, too. Mavis embroidered words and little animals on some.

All her quilts were important to Mavis. Into the patchwork, she put her children's outgrown baby frocks, mixing the pieces with the garments of her dead mother and sister, tying the patterns together finally with the plaid and calico she wore to play-parties and to church as a little girl.

Into the sewing, too, went all her moods of sadness and joy, of bone-tired winter weariness and springtime outbursts of exuberance. In the stitches pulled tight and perfectly knotted were echoes of stories and gossip being swapped. In those pieces of cloth were sewn her secret dreams and ambitions, her private thoughts.

It wasn't just an old woman's hope of heavenly rescue layered into her quilting. There were pieces of cloth hiding restrained hints of sex and outright sin. The time Mavis saw the Foute boys bathing naked in the creek, she came home and embroidered little winged honeybees into a piece of yellow cloth, the piercing needle like a silver stinger slipping in and out of the material at hand.

Her favorite quilt was the Cussing Cover. She and her husband only used it on the very coldest nights. It was their last resort to keep from catching the shivers when the winter wind blew through the cabin seams and it was cold enough to freeze your toes to the floor.

All the rash anger of a young married couple was stitched into that quilt. The first year she was married, Basil's mother made him three new shirts for his birthday. One was red. The first day that he wore it, he and Mavis fell into an awful argument about what church to go to on Christmas. She was Primitive Baptist, and Basil didn't take to the preacher there.

Mavis wouldn't budge on the issue. She told him she wasn't going to Christmas church anywhere else. If he were dead, Basil wouldn't sit still to listen to that preacher, not one minute. And he let her know it in a blue streak of cuss words she hadn't heard before. He wore that red shirt and shouted cusses up one side of the house and down the other until she didn't think there would be Christmas at all.

It was the first time he wore the red shirt and the last. When Basil took it off, Mavis slipped it away and went at it with the scissors. It eventually showed up in a quilt pattern of little red squares between the bigger pieces. She backed it with her wedding white, which she'd thought would be curtains, but was too plain, really, once she took that dress apart.

Yet it always remained her favorite quilt. The one with the little red squares in it would keep you warm to 20-below, she reckoned, and that was after she'd forgotten some of the cuss words he'd shouted at her. But, oh, they were the powerful ones, that was for certain, direct references to the violent moods and emotions that angered men are capable of feeling.

Mavis caught her death a little sooner than some. When she was sick, the only thing she cared about was that Basil keep her quilts from the antiquers who had started coming into the mountains and buying up everything that mattered to anyone.

"You must keep my quilts in the family," she said. "And you promise me never to put a one of them on a metal bed. Not a one."

Basil agreed. There was so much of Mavis in her quilts that she feared they would share the same fate as a baby born during a thunderstorm.

"When you marry another woman, you give my quilts to the children," Mavis instructed. "And you have them swear an oath not to put them on a metal bed. You'll do that for me, Basil, won't you?"

He said he would and asked her not to be speaking of another woman.

Basil said it tore at his heart to have her thinking it.

Some men are born lonely and can't live a day without somebody around. Basil must have been one of them. He took up with Trulie Jane Lawson within a year after Mavis was buried. Trulie was hugely fat and had never once been accused of beauty. She was simple, people said. More than all that, she was fifteen years old.

Basil, who was an old man, told everyone he couldn't do any better and took Trulie to church and married her. Trulie's folks didn't mind. There wasn't much she could do. Basil had to teach her to make biscuits. She couldn't sew a lick, but Trulie was warm to sleep with, and she listened to everything Basil said.

When she asked him to buy her a new bed, Basil said he figured he would. Trulie was a big, round woman of a girl, and she wanted a bed with a metal frame and metal springs. Basil said it was okay by him, and he bought her one with the money he earned by selling off trees to the lumbermen.

Despite his promise to Mavis, Basil kept the quilts his wife had made. Trulie couldn't sew her own, and winters are cold in Cades Cove. You couldn't blame him for keeping the covers, even though he was breaking another promise by putting them on the metal bed. A big, soft woman can keep an old man from freezing on a winter night, but what keeps her warm are covers. Trulie favored the quilt with the little red squares on top and the plain white backing.

Trulie put the Cussing Cover on the bed and climbed in. Basil climbed in after her.

"What was that!" Trulie said in the middle night, sitting up in bed. "Wake up, Basil! Wake up, darn it!"

Basil came awake.

"What is it, Trulie?"

"An old woman is cussing at me. Can't you hear it?"

"No." He hadn't heard anything.

"Well, she's still doing it! Listen!"

Basil listened. "I don't hear anything," he finally said. "Maybe it's thunder on Gregory Bald."

Trulie waited, her mouth twisted into a fist of concentration. She didn't like being cussed at by a ghost. Trulie had seen her, but didn't say anything to Basil, just in case she was imagining things.

Mavis stood at the foot of the bed, wearing a flimsy, white robe. It was far too little clothing to be wearing at night in winter. The old woman's hair was hanging down loose, as if she'd been combing it. She stood at the foot of the bed, cussing at Trulie and Basil. He couldn't hear her, although she was awfully loud. The old woman's eyes sparkled like stars.

"It's over now," Trulie said, hoping that it was. "Like to scared me to my grave, Basil. If that was your old wife, I want you to tell her to stop it. You tell her I'm here now. This is my bed, and you are my man."

"I'll do that," Basil said. He went back to sleep.

"See that you do," Trulie said, pulling the covers up to her chins.

Basil woke up five minutes later when he heard something big and sudden. It seemed to him like he saw something, too—something bright and quick and all around him. He went back over his entire life in his head and thought, *Now, isn't that strange?* Each time he remembered something he'd done when he was little, he could smell sulfur. He could smell meat burning, too. Then, a searing heat flashed across his entire body, and Basil thought he might be on fire. It was the last thought he had.

Trulie came flying out of that cabin in a fast trot, looking for help from someone somewhere. She'd been knocked from the bed in one big wallop, she said. "I saw the flames rise up behind me, and I got up and started moving," Trulie told her pa.

The men in Trulie's family stuck their feet into boots and hurried back to Basil's cabin, figuring to put out the fire if there was anything left of the cabin by then. Her father climbed on his mule and kicked it right along at a fair pace. When he arrived at the cabin on Whistling Branch, it was still standing and a small tail of smoke lifted from the chimney.

From the path to the house it looked like nothing was out of the ordinary. Trulie's brothers were there shortly. One of them saw the big, square hole in the roof. The hole had been burnt there, directly over the couples' bed.

Inside, they found Basil. He'd been cooked by a fire, which seemed limited to the bed. The bed was also cooked away to nothing but black ashes. The metal frame had melted through the puncheon floorboards, which had caught fire in the shape of the bed and burned through to the ground. The boards under the bed were smoldering coals in straight lines on the earth under the big hole in the floor.

Nothing else caught fire from the lightning strike.

"Came down through the roof," Trulie's father said. "Must have been a small thundercloud that come by."

People in the area remembered hearing a clap of thunder that night, but no one had rain in the entire cove. Trulie's father and her two brothers looked up through the hole in the roof of Basil's cabin at a perfectly clear night sky painted with stars. It was cold in the cabin with the roof open. One of Trulie's brothers grabbed a folded quilt from the corner of the room and shook it open to wrap it around his shoulders for the walk home. It was the white-backed quilt with small red squares between the bigger pieces of the pattern.

"Leave that be," his father said. "Mavis made them covers. They belong to her kin."

Although he was clearly struck by lightning while he lay asleep safe and sound in his own bed, everybody said Basil Estep's first wife killed him. And the people in Cades Cove knew why.

Mavis's eldest daughter sold her mother's quilts to an antiquer. She said she needed the money. Could be that she was afraid of them.

Cades Cove, Tennessee, first settled in 1821, has been absorbed by the Great Smoky Mountains National Park. Cattle graze the pastures of the pleasant valley community. The park maintains some of the houses, barns, cemeteries, churches, and a mill at the site as a living exhibit.

Visitors to Cades Cove today find an eleven-mile one-way road that circles the cove. There are nineteen stops along the way to explain a uniquely American way of life from a century before. Some people ride bicycles along the trail.

There are antique stores throughout the area that specialize in local craft items—handmade furniture, musical instruments, pottery, basketry, loom work, and rugs. Hand-pieced quilts are highly valued, especially those that have outlived the loving hands that made them. Should you visit antique stores in eastern Tennessee, it might be wise to avoid bringing home an antique quilt with white backing that has little red squares between the larger pieces of the quilted pattern. Or if you do, please don't place the Cussing Cover on a bed with a metal frame or springs.

A Vampire Chair

*H*andmade sitting chairs have long been a staple of the antique and crafts business in rural, wooded communities. When Allen Eaton published *Handicrafts of the Southern Highlands* in 1937, there were several noted chair makers in eastern Tennessee. Mary Ownby, of Gatlinburg, was a highlight of Eaton's book. She crafted her chairs from beginning to end. Mary's first step in making a chair was finding the right tree, which she cut herself. She then split the wood and turned the posts.

Mary made her own chisels. And, like other chair makers, she bragged that she had made her first chair with a pocketknife.

Other well-respected chair crafters in the 1930s were Ebb Bowman, hard at work in Greeneville, and Noah McCarter in Sevierville. Along with those produced by Mary Ownby, Bowman and McCarter chairs are highly prized by today's collectors.

Long before the craftsmen of the 1930s began to put together chairs, other southern chair makers had adapted the standard slat-back chair into an item distinct from manufactured Hitchcock chairs. The rear posts were shaved down and curved backwards. The result was a seat that folks now call a mule-ear chair. It is similar to the type made in the early 1800s.

Sometimes there were two slats across the back, sometimes three.

But the most famous handcrafted sitting chair made in the region hasn't been located recently. When it is found, you don't want to be the one sitting in it. The chair is cursed in a peculiar way and is apt to draw blood.

A true antique, the so-called Vampire Chair of East Tennessee was made by brothers named Eli and Jacob Odom up in the high mountains of Carter County near Shell Creek. The brothers seem to be of no relation to Solomon W. Odom, a highly regarded former chair maker in the same area.

Eli and Jacob Odom came to Shell Creek in 1806, it is believed, and began making chairs that they traded for salt, sugar, meat, and coffee. The brothers knew that a chair was only as good as its joints, and they had a secret for making perfect joints. They carefully fitted seasoned hickory rounds into green maple posts. The green wood shrunk over the rounds as it dried, holding them tightly into place. Old wood into new, that was all there was to it.

The brothers' chairs became famous because they held together so well. Hundreds of chairs were made and traded. By the 1840s, the chairs Eli and Jacob made were being carried down the mountain and taken into stores where they were sold for hefty profit. Resort hotels lined their long front porches with the mule-ear chairs from Shell Creek.

Wagonloads of the chairs were eventually driven south and the slat-back seats of Carter County found their way into the finer homes of Chattanooga.

Through normal trade, a pair of chairs made their way into the domicile of a woman who lived alone in a little cabin high above the Hiwassee River near Charleston, Tennessee. This woman was nobody's sweet little old lady. The woman who lived high on a cliff above the river was a vampire.

There is no record of her exploits, nor of the reasons her neighbors held for killing her. All that is known is how she died and where she was buried.

In 1917, a county crew was widening the upper road on the river bluff just outside Charleston. Not far from Oostanaula Creek, they unearthed the body of an adult woman who had been buried long before.

She'd been buried, apparently, in the middle of the road. The body, according to the late Frank G. Trewhitt, was wholly petrified by the high level of minerals in the ground water there.

Also petrified was the wooden stake that had been driven through the woman's heart prior to her body being buried in the road.

"The land on which the body was found was once the property of my great grandfather, and it was passed to his sons," Mr. Trewhitt wrote in an article published in the *Tennessee Folklore Society Bulletin.* "If they had ever heard of any vampire stories hereabouts, I would have been told."

It was once tradition to refuse sanctified burials to known murderers, witches, and other perceived villains of society. Scoundrels and witches were at times buried at crossroads, so that their eternal rest would be anything but peaceful. It was the practice to bury evil persons where foot, horse, and wagon traffic would create a continual clamor overhead.

Traffic would also keep the dirt above the grave tightly packed down. This is important, particularly with vampires and witches. Such evildoers might be able to return from the dead and escape their coffins by tooth and fingernail, clawing their way to the surface to seek revenge.

As an additional measure of safety, these ghouls, once executed, were buried face down. Should they wake from death interred and seek to dig themselves from under the earth, they would dig in the wrong direction. They would only dig themselves more deeply into the earth.

The piece of wood through the dust-dry heart of the mummified corpse of Bradley County's lady vampire wasn't any old piece of wood. It was a cradle-lathed post, a bottom leg support, from one of the chairs that had been in the woman's cabin on the ridge. The chair had been crafted by brothers Eli and Jacob from Shell Creek.

Soon after her murder and burial, the woman's furniture and other worthwhile belongings were carried from her home by those who desired them. The house fell to ruin. Nobody would live there.

It wasn't long until the Eli and Jacob chair, its round expertly replaced, found its way into a prompt series of trades among the citizens of Bradley County. No one wanted to keep that chair. After a few years, it ended up at one of the hotels. Someone, who was afraid to throw away or light fire to it, left it on the hotel's porch at the end of a line of similarly made chairs.

Legend says the chair sits as comfortably as any, with a finely woven seat of hickory splits. Well, at first. Then it becomes very uncomfortable for the person who sits in the chair.

Nothing is seen, but plenty is felt. The occupant is held fast for a time, against one's will, until a scratch appears on a forearm or bare leg, and blood drips to the floor. Only after a drop of blood stains the floor or the ground under the chair, is the occupant capable of fleeing from the chair.

Those familiar with the blood-drawing qualities of this individual chair were afraid to destroy it, beat it to pieces with hammers, or catch it on fire, lest they be cursed in a manner much worse than a drop of blood hitting the floor. So they passed it along.

The Eli and Jacob Odom handcrafted slat-back chair haunts eastern Tennessee still. Reports have placed it in any number of antique stores over the years. Others have sworn it was once on the creaky front porch of a bed-and-breakfast in Gatlinburg, on the college campus at Tusculum, and at a garage sale in Kingsport. Truth is the Vampire Chair of East Tennessee could turn up just about anywhere. The hope remains that it doesn't turn up perched under you.

The Granny Curse

*T*he stem between her teeth, Cassie held the red-ripe apple in her hand and turned it to the left, like turning a doorknob. Each time she turned the apple, she repeated a letter of the alphabet to herself, starting with *A*. The stem always came away from an apple on the letter *H*. Every time.

It was the initial of the man she would marry. Cassie knew it to be true. It had been that way since she was ten years old and played in the big oak tree with Hodge.

Hodge Hendricks Harrison lived with his family way back on a heavily wooded and rocky hill over toward the mountains. His grandma lived in the house with them. This was just east of Knoxville, near a southern bend in the French Broad River. There has never been a town there.

The oak tree was old and tall. It shaded the big spring that some folks called Dark Morning Spring. The little stream of water that ran off from it was Dark Morning Creek. Moss grew by the spring. So did clover. So did mint. Of course, there were acorns. Acorns were everywhere, that year's acorns and those from seasons past. When the caps fell into the spring upside down, they floated like boats along Dark Morning Creek. Cassie picked clover flowers and put a flower in an acorn cap and sent it off on the water like a ship to sea.

Hodge was only eleven himself, or maybe twelve, when he first showed up at the spring. He walked toward her, walked in the middle of the creek with his shoes thrown over his shoulder, their laces tied together in a bowknot, his bare feet in the cold water. He reached down and picked up the little boat Cassie had made, an acorn cap with a clover flower inside. It floated right to him.

When Hodge picked it up, Cassie knew then that they would be married. She knew it on the spot.

Until he showed up Cassie had thought the tree was all hers. She didn't mind sharing it. Hodge was taller and could reach the lowest limb without having to jump. He could climb nearly as well as she could. But not quite.

They played there nearly every day, unless it rained or was too cold in winter. Some days Hodge would show up as it was getting dark and could only stay a moment, stay just long enough to poke a stick in the water or pluck a sprig of mint. He'd smile at her for a minute, no more than that. A honeybee might have time to circle his head, and then he was off. There was always work for Hodge to do at home once his daddy died.

When her father said she shouldn't play with that boy, Cassie didn't know exactly what he meant.

"He doesn't go to the Baptist church," her mother said.

"Maybe no one asked him," Cassie told her mother. And when Cassie invited him to come, Hodge showed up that Sunday at church. The home-weave shirt he wore was clean, but worn through in several spots. Not all the buttons matched. Hodge sat in the back pew, embarrassed for the poor condition of his only pair of shoes.

His grandma had taught Hodge church songs at home. He knew most of the words and sang along with the rest of them. Cassie loved him for that, even though his voice had more holes in it than his shirt.

Up the hollow, behind the big oak tree, above the spring, Cassie helped Hodge find herbs. And butterflies. Hodge knew heartsease and ginseng from his grandma and taught Cassie where to find it. He knew where most of the herbs grew and what every one was used for. He told her that butterflies were messengers and so were bees and when one of them landed on you it meant something good would happen.

They fell in love. It came to Cassie like a bee and landed on her. She knew she was going to marry him anyway, because every time she turned an apple stem in her teeth it came out on the letter *H*.

Her father saw them together again and told Cassie that he wouldn't allow her to be in company of that boy.

"He's a nice boy, Daddy," she said. Cassie held a big secret in her heart.

"Nice doesn't matter," her father said. "His family's no good. His grandmother's a witch."

"It's not true," she said. Her father saying it made her cry. "She's not a witch, Daddy. She's just a granny woman. She makes folks medicines and such from plants."

"That's not what I hear," he said. "And that's that."

Cassie ran outside. She ran to the tree by Dark Morning Spring and cried. She picked up an acorn cap and scraped the edge of it up along her cheek, catching a teardrop. She put it in the spring, a little round boat with her tear inside, and off it went. It was her messenger.

Hodge came. It was after dark. He came to the door and stood on the wooden stoop and knocked bravely until Cassie's mother answered it and, being polite, she invited him inside.

Hodge spoke to Cassie's father. Hodge's face was red with fear. His hands shook.

"I am here," Hodge said, "to ask the father's permission to court his daughter." He looked directly at Cassie's dad.

"No," was all her father said.

Cassie heard him say it. She didn't leave the house for a week. She didn't go to church Sunday, neither morning church nor night. That afternoon, her parents had the preacher over to the house for dinner.

"The Lord will bring you another man," the preacher said. "The Lord will bring you a better man, one that will please you and your parents."

Cassie didn't want another man. She wanted the one she already loved and who loved her back.

It was autumn, and night fell early. The moon was large and yellow.

You could see it low to the trees. It was sitting on the ridge just above the spring.

Cassie knew her wish. And she knew how to make her wish come true. The old folks called it *drinking the moon*. It was what she set out to do.

She needed a silver bowl or silver cup for drinking the moon. It had to be silver. No other metal would qualify. It had to be silver to have her wish come true. She couldn't find one. There were no silver dishes in her parent's house. Cassie wondered where she might go to borrow a silver bowl, then remembered just in time that her mother had a large silver spoon at the back of a cedar box in the kitchen. It would have to do.

She left the house with the spoon and made her way to the spring. Leaves had fallen from the oak tree. The moon was full. It had to be full for drinking the moon. And she had to be very careful to do it just right. You only got one wish this way. She stepped from the night shadow of the tall oak and knelt by the spring. Cassie caught a big mouthful of clear water in the silver spoon.

Careful not to spill a drop, she lifted the spoon in front of her. Ever so slowly, she brought it to a place where, when she held it just so and held it steady, she could see the perfect reflection of the full moon in the water. The water worked like a mirror.

Cassie made her wish. She made it hard and deep. Then she brought her mouth to the spoon, holding it where the moon was sitting in the water like a round light, and she drank it in a single swallow—the water and the moon. Her wish would come true.

The next day she met Hodge and told him what she'd done. They agreed to wait a month and see what happened. He believed in things magical. People who live in the mountains often do.

He came to Cassie's house when the moon was full again, when her wish might best be granted, and knocked on the door in early evening. It was cold out. Smoke rose from the chimney. It looked warm inside. But this time Cassie's parents didn't let Hodge come in. Her father met him at the door and told the young man to go away.

"There is nothing you can do to change my mind," her father said.

Cassie heard him say it, and she cried.

Two days later she found Hodge sitting on the hill behind the spring. He told her what to do next.

"Your magic didn't do the trick," he said.

"Maybe it takes more time. Maybe it takes a year."

"Maybe it takes a hundred years," Hodge told her. "I don't feel like waiting a hundred years, do you?"

Cassie shook her head no.

"I talked to my granny. She told me what to do."

"Quick, tell me!" Cassie begged. "I have to go back soon."

"Take this with you and put it under the step to your front door." Hodge handed her a little bundle of hair from a horse's tail, tied with a piece of wool thread.

"What is it?" It felt strange to Cassie. It felt scratchy and empty inside when she closed her hand over it.

"That's a horsehair ball my granny fixed up. It's a curse, Cassie, to have your parents let us be married."

She put the witch bundle where he told her to. Cassie hoped it worked. She thought maybe her parents would catch a cough or have headaches or be unable to sleep. That was the nature of curses most folks blamed on witches. Or maybe the cream wouldn't rise to the top of the milk, or the churn would no longer make butter. Cassie hoped her parents didn't catch fits. And she certainly didn't want to see her mother and father turned into cats.

The next morning, Cassie stepped outside for fresh kindling to stoke the fire. When she came back inside, stepping over the witch bundle, she caught the curse, caught it as surely as if she had been bitten by a snake. But she didn't know it until her mother spoke to her next.

When Cassie opened her mouth to reply, not a word came out. Not a word that her mother could hear. Instead, Cassie's body made another noise. She vented intestinal gas with a persistent rumbling low in her belly, then emitted a series of popping sounds from the same source. It was long and it was loud.

"Heavens to Betsy Ross," her mother said. "Are you sick? Are you alright?"

Cassie felt fine. She started to tell her mother so. But again, whenever she tried to speak, her body vented gas—from the area of the human body that leaves the room last when a person walks out the door. It was as long and as loud as before. Cassie had to snap her mouth tightly shut to get the behind part of her body to stop it. So powerful and sudden an outburst of gas it was that she feared the force of it might rip a hole in the seam of her bloomers.

Her mother stepped outside to catch her breath and to keep from scolding her daughter for something the young lady obviously could not control. When she stepped back into the house, she caught the curse herself.

She meant to tell Cassie that maybe a kettle of fresh water from the spring would be of benefit. When the older woman opened her mouth to speak, a bit of wind escaped her body's lower vent as well. It began as no more than a squeak like that of a mouse. Then a bit more broke free. Then more still. The squeak turned into a trumpeting.

Being much larger than her daughter, the music her body played was not limited to that of a single instrument. Or species. Her sound had definite range, coupled with an aggressive personality. Near the end, you would have thought the room was filled with the hollering of migrating geese, mixed with the lonely cackle of a fattened turkey hen.

The unsavory noise brought Cassie's father downstairs in a rush. He glowered at the ladies of the domicile. Both began to speak at once, in an attempt to apologize or explain. Their shared attempt failed as wind expelled itself unceasingly from below their waists. They could have died of embarrassment. Cassie was so shaken by the reflex trumpeting of her body that she failed to realize this was the effect of the granny curse.

Cassie's father, having taken in the scent of the situation, rushed at once from the room. He strode out the front door, picked up the small bucket for carrying water, and hurried to the spring. He did not know the name of the illness that had overcome his household, but if fresh water didn't help the two of them, he would mount his horse and fetch the preacher to come to the house and pray for them.

Returning with spring water, he clambered over the front steps and into the house, of a mind to tell the women what he was set to do. Instead of words, when he opened his mouth to talk, he heard and felt a low rumbling, a resounding roll from well below his navel. The rumbling changed into a tattoo of steady thunder as gas sought and found rearward escape from his body. The water in the pail whitecapped. It was a seemingly endless, large and jarring stampede of angry noise, befitting the head of the house. You'd have thought that old oak tree out back had come crashing down.

Windows were opened.

Eventually, an uncertain ease was upon the home as the three family members staunchly refrained from any attempt to utter a thought. As long as they did not try to speak, their bodies behaved without eruption, without wind. The season was too cold for the windows to be left open and, as peace settled upon the household, each window in turn was eased shut.

They would have eaten breakfast but had lost their appetites. Before one of them figured out they could slip outdoors to talk uninterrupted, Hodge showed up in the yard.

He called to the house. No one answered.

Hodge ambled forward, reaching the front step. Leaning over the wooden steps, and not walking across the witch ball, he knocked on the door.

"Hello," he called. "Hello! Anybody home?"

There was no reply.

For a moment there he thought he heard a voice, then heard what sounded like someone scooting a table across the floor. Then he heard a window being lifted. He hurried to it.

Hodge stuck his head inside the window. "Good morning to you, ma'am. Good morning to you, sir." He smiled at each of them in turn. "And an especially good morning to you, my honey lamb." He grinned at Cassie. She smiled back.

Her suitor reached his arm in through the window.

"If there be no spoken objection, I come to seek your daughter's hand in marriage. For the third time, which is I understand by all protocol accepted by civilized men the final time I may ask." He stretched his hand out to Cassie, who leapt to her feet and rushed to take it in her own.

"If you will, my love." Hodge said. "But answer with your eyes," he was quick to add.

Cassie beamed great joy at him and nodded her head vigorously.

"What's that then?" Hodge continued. "Neither parent speaks to disagree?"

The handsome young man released Cassie's hand, and she hurried across the room and out the door to be swept up in his waiting arms. Her father made some noises at this point, but nothing you could understand, nothing that would hold up in court, and nothing he cared to repeat to anyone. The lovers were away and soon married. They told the preacher they had her father's blessing.

The preacher knew Cassie never to lie. He asked her if it were true. "It was the third time he asked, and Papa didn't say a word against it," she vowed, her hand upon the Holy Bible. Soon she was pronounced Mrs. Hodge Hendricks Henderson.

The young married couple returned to the house near Dark Morning Spring, and the groom removed the small bundle of horsehair from under the stoop. With the granny bundle tucked safely into his pocket, Hodge whooped and hollered. He shouted for Cassie's parents to come outside and greet the new bride in the family.

Sheepishly, they appeared, one behind the other, Cassie's mother first. As they stepped out the door of the house, the curse was lifted, never to visit the home again. Cassie's parents came to say over the years that, as any respectable parents might choose to do, they had waited until Hodge had asked the third time before permitting their only child to marry him. Hodge's grandma never believed a word of it.

In the days that followed, whenever Cassie placed a stem between her teeth and turned the apple attached to it like a doorknob, it always came free on the letter *H*. Just as it ever did. Only this time it was *H* for Harry, if her firstborn were to be a boy. Or *H* for Hodgeleeanna Bea should her first child be born to wear pink. She wouldn't be sure for awhile yet.

Letitita Edes Mountain

Of course the mountains are alive. They're covered with living forests, with all sizes of plants and flowers, from modest herbs and hidden mushrooms to clustered canes of blueberries and flamboyant displays of brilliant rhododendron.

The rising peaks and plunging valleys teem with wildlife. More than two hundred species of birds thrive in the forests of the Cumberland and the Blue Ridge Mountains. Chipmunks and squirrels likely exist in numbers larger than the count of people who live in the mountains, not to mention moths and millipedes, bats and bears, rabbits and deer.

The mountains are a composition of endless life, from the gentle trickle of streams over mossy rocks to raging river torrents, from the striped salamander to the sudden appearance of man. The mountains were home to unknown races of people long before the arrival of the Cherokee. The soul of both live on in the mountains, as does the spirit of the mountain pioneers.

But sometimes even the mountains themselves are alive. For example, there's Letitia Edes Mountain, a mountain that was once a woman who wouldn't stop growing. Letitia Edes was first brought to the attention of outsiders through the published works of Mildred Haun, a Tennessee author who was a member of a distinct racial group, commonly called Melungeons.

Melungeons were known to be living in eastern Tennessee as early as the 1790s. While everyone agrees they came from somewhere else, nobody knows where they came from. For the longest time, they were believed to be of Portuguese descent, but with a mixture of other races, perhaps Native American, perhaps Afro-American.

Many Melungeons described themselves as Portuguese at times of census taking in the early nineteenth century, seemingly accepting the theory that they were descendants of a Portuguese ship's crew. When the ship foundered and sank off the coast of North Carolina, the crew moved inland and, being all men, took wives from among the native population, settling in the lush river valley east of the Cumberland Mountains.

Others proposed that the generally dark-skinned, dark-haired Melungeons might be the direct descendants of the Lost Colony of Roanoke Island. The colony disappeared from the coastal island about twenty years before the English established the first permanent settlement at Jamestown. John White, the governor of the island colony, went back to England for two years. When he returned, the people he'd left in America had vanished.

A romantic notion is that the colony, pressed by starvation, moved west, commingling with Native Americans, and became the forebears of the Melungeons. Proponents of this idea offer as evidence the large number of common English last names among the Melungeons.

Under any circumstances, the Melungeons were racially distinct from later white settlers who moved into the fertile farmland. The Melungeons, discriminated against by white settlers, had their land taken by laws similar to those that took land from the Cherokee. The 1834 Tennessee Constitutional Convention established the status of Melungeon people as free persons of color. Being *of color* was a legal distinction that deprived people of their right to vote, to own land, and to bring (or answer) suit in court.

Their homes stolen, the Melungeons were pushed out. They relocated in the unclaimed and harsher landscapes of the area, making their new homes well back in the rugged hollows and ridges of the nearby mountains. For more than a century the Melungeons lived in isolation and poverty.

Few knew how to read and write at the time of the publication of American racial summaries compiled by W. H. Gilbert for the Library of Congress in 1968. Gilbert noted that the highest concentration of the

Melungeons was at Newman's Ridge in Hancock County. Melungeon population centers were also noted at Clinch Mountain and Copper Ridge, with dispersed populations in eighteen counties in eastern Tennessee.

Gilbert went on to describe the Melungeon dwellings as crude, suggesting that some families live in dugout holes in the sides of cliffs. While he credited the Melungeons with possessing organized religious faith, either that of the Presbyterians or the Baptists, Gilbert concluded his report with a single notation of what he called a "cultural peculiarity," saying that a belief in magic and folklore seemed important to them.

Indeed, a rich body of distinctly Melungeon folklore was developed and nurtured over many years of cultural isolation and racial discrimination. There were no trained doctors for these communities. Much of the Melungeon magic involved cures and treatments for illness or injury. Herbs were commonly used to stop bleeding, as were secret sayings.

An individual in the Melungeon community who could shout the right words to cause a wound to seal was known as a *blood stopper* and highly valued among his neighbors. Blood stoppers received their secret instructions from someone of the opposite sex or the charm would fail. A baby's sore throat was treated by having an adult son who had never seen his own father (by the father having died or otherwise abandoned the family before his son's birth), blow into the baby's mouth.

Oftentimes, an older woman of remote Appalachian communities, known as a granny woman, assisted with births. Possessing more than a passing knowledge of herbal remedies, a granny woman provided treatment for sickness. And she would prepare the dead for burial when called upon. Though a respected member of the community, a granny woman was often thought of as a witch.

Much Melungeon folklore, in which life is never easy, deals with death. It is a harsh folk tradition found among a people forced to live a harsh existence. Yet, there is celebration in the folklore as well. Along with many of the impoverished mountain backwoods people, the Melungeons had moonshine and music.

Perhaps the Melungeon best known to outsiders is Mahala Mullins. She is famous in history and in folklore for being arrested for selling moonshine, but never apprehended. Her reputation looms as large as myth, which is not inappropriate to her own proportions. An existing photograph of Mahala in later life offers evidence that those who estimated her weight at five hundred pounds were not far off.

Known as Big Haley, Mahala raised fourteen children. She and her husband grew apples and sold cider on Newman's Ridge. They also operated a still.

Eventually arrested by federal revenue agents for selling unlicensed and untaxed homemade whiskey, Mahala Mullins stood her ground. And stood her ground. And stood her ground. In fact, she was never taken into custody because she could not be removed from her house. Mahala would not fit through the door of her log cabin. The federal agents were forced to leave her there.

Mahala never saw court. She died at home. As in life, it proved impossible to remove her body through any window or door of her sturdy mountain cabin. The stones of the fireplace had to be knocked down to find a portal large enough for the removal of the body.

There also exists another Melungeon woman known for her size, a woman as large as a mountain—literally.

In 1940, Mildred Haun published *The Hawks Done Gone*, a haunting collection of short stories set in the eastern Tennessee mountains. The work contains a virtually complete catalog of superstitions in the southern Appalachians. In the prologue to her stories, Haun introduces the world to Letitia Edes Mountain, which rises up large and tall between other peaks of the Cumberland range in Hancock County. The mountain, even then, could be seen from far, far away.

Letitia Edes didn't start out as a mountain. She was a Melungeon girl born at midnight on Old Christmas. Also known as Twelfth Day, old Christmas falls on January 6. It is a special time when the spiritual world holds dominion over the earth. At midnight on old Christmas, cattle kneel down in the fields to pray, and their voices can be heard to speak.

People born at midnight on Twelfth Day are destined, one way or another, to never die. Their spirits live on among us, each continuing to do after death what they were doing in real life.

In real life Letitia Edes ate. Then ate some more. Of the four basic needs of a pioneer family in Appalachia—food, clothing, shelter, and fuel—Letitia's greatest attention was given to food.

She liked everything from the garden. Cabbage, lettuce, radishes, cucumbers, okra, tomatoes, beans, and peas. She liked everything from the fields—sweet potatoes, Irish potatoes, corn, pumpkins, squash, turnips, mustard greens, and popcorn. Letitia liked to eat apples, peaches, pears, cherries, berries, plums, and grapes. She liked bread and pie and pancakes. Biscuits and gravy, too.

Oh, she enjoyed eating honey. And Letitia liked meat. Her favorites were pork and beef. Chickens fried and stewed. And rabbit, squirrel, bear, deer, possum, and coon. Not to mention owl soup. She'd eat frog legs, to boot.

She was a big girl, and later a big woman. A very big woman. Folks say that as an adult she still grew an inch a year because of her devotion to her one true calling—the consumption of food. When she died, Letitia Edes was very large indeed.

Because of the mountain rocks and tree roots, no one could dig a hole big enough for Letitia's body. The men would have broken every pick and shovel they could lay hands to and yet not have a hole in the ground half big enough to receive her body. And she didn't look to be getting any smaller dead. So, Letitia's body was laid out in the yard for a day or two, under the shade of a couple of trees. They tied her mouth shut with a tablecloth to keep the bees out.

Waiting wouldn't do. You couldn't let somebody sit around dead in the long heat of summer.

With the help of a team of horses, the men managed to move her body off into a low meadow between two hills. They covered her with dirt. Ladies from the church sang hymns. The men covered the first layer of dirt with two more layers of rocks. It took two days to finish the task. They made a mound of Letitia Edes.

The mound soon became a small mountain. No one noticed right off, but Letitia Edes continued to grow in death, as she had in life, an inch a year. Pretty soon she grew some trees.

Nobody knows for sure what year she died, but she's a fully mature mountain now. Letitia Edes Mountain rises above many others in Hancock County. On a perfectly clear day, you can see it from between the peaks of nearer mountains from just about anywhere in the area. Hikers who have made their way to Letitia Edes Mountain say that you can feel the mountain breathe. They say you can hear it breathing, too. And when they speak of the mountain being alive, they mean it in a whole different way than with your other mountains in Tennessee.

The Secrets of Apples and Oaks

*T*he heart of a forest, the soul of an orchard, is a solitary tree. Trees throughout eastern Tennessee hold secrets both ancient and modern. Some secrets, such as the names that correspond to the initials of lovers carved into a tree, are visible to the casual passerby. Other secrets lie fixed within the woody core of a tree, or entangled with particles of moist dirt among a tree's ever-seeking, ever-deepening roots.

Great forests once covered most of Tennessee. Only a tiny fraction remain. What virgin timber that does exist is likely hardwood—a massive old oak, a stately elm, or perhaps a giant beech. Stands of old-timber hemlock, pine, spruce, and Fraser firs are found in eastern Tennessee as the altitude increases.

Maple and cherry trees are not rare, nor are sweet gum, poplar, willow, and sycamore. In the mountainous reaches of the eastern part of the state, rhododendron grows to the height of trees and can be found in seemingly unending thickets that are known to cover an entire mountainside. In the Great Smoky Mountains National Park alone more species of trees thrive than can be found in all of Europe.

Trees provide part of the landscape that contributes to the history of Tennessee. The first settlers made their homes from trees. Winter was survived by chopping down trees and burning the logs in fireplaces. Sometimes, even a more basic form of shelter figured in the history of pioneers on the frontier of eastern Tennessee. One of the early settlers to the area, it is recorded, survived the severe winter of 1779 by living in the hollow trunk of a large oak tree.

Pine knots were often burned, in place of candles, as an economical and readily available source of light.

Many early settlers brought a mysterious understanding of the secrets of the forest with them when they came to Tennessee. For example, in August the forest floor heats with verdant life. On the twenty-first of the month, it is said the trees place words upon the breeze. It is considered unwise to enter the woods on this date because of the things you will hear. It is then that the trees whisper your future and the futures of all your friends and acquaintances.

There are also secrets to be found among apple trees. A young girl in a homesteader's family in eastern Tennessee didn't have to wait until the twenty-first of August to hear her future whispered between forest leaves in the dark woods. She could discover her future by eating an apple and counting the seeds. And she still can today.

The code was once passed orally from generation to generation as a rhyme. The secret code, as it was told in eastern Tennessee, was collected and preserved by folklorists working in the nineteenth century. Using the following code that corresponds to the entire number of seeds in an apple, you can learn your future. However, the apple must be completely eaten for one's future to come true.

> One through three are love, they say.
> Four, you love with all your heart.
> Five, she casts the man away.
> Six, he loves. Seven, she loves. Eight, both love.
> Nine, he comes on time. Ten, he's late.
> Eleven, he courts. Twelve, he marries.
> Thirteen, you quarrel. Fourteen, you part.

Fifteen, you die of a broken heart.
Sixteen, kisses. Seventeen, riches.
All the rest are ugly witches.

It's obvious that eating an apple can give you more than nourishment for the body. When you count the seeds against the rhyme above, you provide a little something for the human heart.

And fruit trees aren't the only trees that provide people with food. Before settlers came over the mountains into Tennessee, Indians native to the area survived starvation during the cruel winters by eating acorns.

Trees were so much a part of frontier life that it was inevitable they would find their way into the region's legends. According to the body of material collected from 1887 to 1890 by James Mooney, the Cherokee believed that the whirlwind lived at the utmost leafy tops of the tallest trees. The whirlwind was often an important messenger in the mythology of the Cherokee.

At the site of a historical marker in Athens, Tennessee, the stories of the English-speaking settlers and the native Cherokee merge. The marker chronicles the legend of Nocatula, a Cherokee woman, and her husband, an English officer who was badly wounded in the Battle of Kings Mountain on October 7, 1780. Their spirits reside nearby.

Cherokee hunters found the soldier in the woods and brought him back to their village. He was near death. Nocatula nursed the soldier back to health and fell in love with him. He loved her and was accepted by the Cherokee as one of their own, with the new name, Connestoga. Both hard workers and amiable, the couple was popular in their village and well respected. They were married.

This didn't sit well with one of the young warriors, who believed it was his duty to repel all intruders upon his lands. This included the English soldiers. And, sadly, it included Connestoga. Without provocation, the Cherokee warrior attacked the Englishman and stabbed him through the throat with a long knife. Connestoga died quickly.

Nocatula's heart was broken. She rushed to her fallen husband's side. Wailing in grief, Nocatula took her own life by plunging a stout flint knife directly into her own beating heart. Their bodies lay together in death.

Nocatula's father placed an acorn into the hand of the slain English soldier. Into his daughter's hand he placed a red hackberry and closed her lifeless fingers over it. The lovers' bodies were buried together in honor of their devotion.

The acorn and the hackberry sprouted. Each sent a shoot up through the soil, seeking light. Within a few seasons, twin trees grew from the same spot, one an oak, the other a twisting hackberry elm. Many years later, a college was built on the site (now Tennessee Wesleyan College), but the trees were left in place. Each class of students coming to the college was told the story of the stately oak and the matching hackberry elm tree.

College girls who brought their boyfriends to the location supposedly enjoyed swift proposals of marriage and were happily married for the rest of their lives when the proposals were accepted. The two trees grew, side by side, their roots entwined, their leaves touching, for more than 150 years. The hackberry elm died in 1945, the oak five years later.

A historical marker re-telling the legend of Nocatula was erected at the site in 1957.

Another tree associated with the 1780 Battle of Kings Mountain is the Pemberton Oak in Sullivan County. The tree, thought to be nearly eight hundred years old, predates Columbus by approximately three hundred years. Known to have been a gathering place for colonial forces on their route to best the British in the Battle of Kings Mountain, Pemberton Oak (also known as Royal Oak) is individually listed in the National Register of Historic Places.

Perhaps the most interesting of Tennessee's oaks, however, is a massive black oak that was cut down in 1896 on the Dave Manning farm, near Bybee, in Cocke County. The tree stood about four hundred yards from the east bank of Clay Creek and was a recognized landmark in its day.

A monarch of a tree, the black oak was thought to have been between two hundred and three hundred years old. It had long stood apart from other trees and was more than twelve feet around until it was brought to the ground under the charge of Lorane Cash in 1896. Mr. Cash's workmen soon had the great tree sawn into thirty-inch blocks from which the boards were made by hand. It was slow, hard work to make boards of the oak blocks.

One of the laborers working on the blocks was startled to discover a lock of black hair in the deep heart of the tree. He shouted to the others, who rushed over just in time to watch the lock of hair turn from jet black to a reddish brown, when it came into contact with air for the first time in more than a century.

This lock of hair was a secret held safe by the black oak for many, many years. The mountain men who uncovered it had no idea what the secret was that they had accidentally revealed. Conflicting theories surfaced. It was obvious to all that the hair was human.

It was not the hair of an old person. It had been placed inside the tree by careful design. An auger hole had been drilled three-quarters of an inch in diameter. The hair was placed inside the hole, as if entombed, and a thick round plug had been hammered into place behind it. The tree had grown a full ten inches beyond the plug. The hair was very, very old.

The child from whom it came had been very young. Students of English folklore may be able to guess the origin of a lock of hair that has been placed at the heart of a tree and then plugged tight. One of the women of the community, well versed in the old ways, eventually revealed the secret meaning of the plugged oak to Lorane Cash and his crew.

It was a commonly held folk belief from the Middle Ages that childhood asthma could be cured by having the child stand by an oak tree while a hole is drilled deep into the tree at the youth's exact height. A lock of the child's hair is cut and placed into the hole, which is then plugged so that no air can penetrate. Once the tree grows over the plug, the disease will disappear.

There was little medical science could do for asthma two hundred years ago, if indeed a doctor could be located on the edge of the American frontier. The lock of hair in the Manning Oak is a poignant reminder of the lengths to which people would go in the hope of securing relief for a suffering family member. It also reminds us of our past closeness to and respect for the green, woodland forces of nature.

Even the wilder forces of nature, such as the crackling, booming rage of thunderstorms, could be transformed and made fit for human use by a big old tree. Toothpicks cut from a tree struck by lightning were once believed to cure toothache.

The trees of the mountainous frontier protected people in many ways—providing the safety of a home with four solid walls, or the heat of a log fire on the coldest wintry night. They were the material for many a hoe handle and homemade chair. Of course, fruit trees provided families with food and drink, apple cider, apple butter, and apple pie (or peach, if you prefer).

But a lock of a child's hair, sealed long ago inside the heart of an age-old oak, is a reminder that trees also supplied us with hope.

Sticky Dog, Long Dog . . . and a Dog That's Always Wet

*T*hree ghost dogs are well-documented in the living history of East Tennessee—Sticky Dog, Long Dog, and a dog that is always wet.

Sticky Dog is always initially seen by children, who then—if they are lucky—bring the sudden appearance of the matted, wandering beast to the immediate attention of a parent or another adult. Horror awaits any child who might actually reach out to touch this dog. Sticky Dog is a most curious and persistent beast of legend and was well known to Tennessee's earliest English pioneers. For more than four hundred years, the unruly animal appears wherever Englishmen settle.

A child in the country might be savaged by a wild dog that the toddler mistakes for a pet. A girl or boy, too young to know better than to approach any dog they see, might contract rabies—and a painful death—by a stray dog carrying the illness. As a result, English children were taught, no matter where on earth they lived, that a dog unknown to them should never be petted, should never be touched. To make sure they didn't forget this lesson, they were told the legend of Sticky Dog—a most fearful danger to children. Although the animal might at first appear friendly and seem lonely for company, Sticky Dog is anything but friendly.

Sticky Dog had no trouble crossing the sea to America. Like all world wanderers, the dog prefers to live just outside of town, on the remote edges of civilization. The rugged outback of the southern Appalachians is a perfect setting for Sticky Dog. Children who live farther from town are more at risk to come upon the four-footed, and sometimes seemingly friendly, hound.

Hikers on the Appalachian Trail have spotted Sticky Dog more than once, usually near rocks and water, at the tops of sheer cliffs, at the edges of rushing water and silent, deep pools.

But Sticky Dog isn't really a dog. He is, in fact, an ancient monster who looks just like a dog and, in many ways, behaves like one. Any strange dog might be Sticky Dog. You can't tell by looking. It doesn't matter the color or the size. Be the critter yellow-haired or black, it might be Sticky Dog. Be it a small, darling type of curly-coated terrier, or a big and friendly natured hound, either might be Sticky Dog.

At all cost and any amount of trouble, once seen Sticky Dog must be avoided. He's a wicked beast.

When you touch Sticky Dog, you can't let go. Even if you only intend to pat him on the head ever so lightly, your hand will stick to the mongrel's coat, and nothing will remove it. Having a hand stuck to his matted fur scares Sticky Dog as much as it does the child, and the dog runs for water. Deep water.

Sticky Dog is an expert swimmer and, once in a pool of water, the dog is able to free itself of the child's hands by drowning the little one. A dead hand, of course, comes instantly unstuck.

Neither should children in groups approach a stray dog in the Tennessee mountains or at the edges of a state park. There have been instances in the past of a large, strong Sticky Dog high-tailing it through the woods, around and over rocks in search of water, with as many as six or seven children stuck to its back—six or seven children never seen alive by their parents again.

Sticky Dog is a legend, handed down by parents and grandparents to the family's little ones as a lesson, plain and simple, to leave all stray dogs be. Long Dog, on the other hand, is the living ghost of a devoted family pet. Long Dog makes her presence known along Tenn. 346 between Surgoinsville and Stony Point. The state highway here follows the path of the Old Stage Road, used as the route to Nashville since the 1790s.

Not many cars drive slowly enough at night on the highway east of Surgoinsville, slowly enough for a dog to trot alongside the car in stride, but sometimes a car will pull over to fix a flat. Then Long Dog appears, running down the middle of the highway. Within moments, the sleek ghost dog is at the windows of any parked car on this stretch of road. She leaps about the stopped vehicle, circling it several times, and eventually climbs onto the hood of the car, from where she peers intently into the car's interior.

Long Dog is looking for someone.

Those who have experienced the roadside visitor report that the white dog, once satisfied that whoever she seeks isn't present, leaps from the car and runs away, back along the highway. They watch her until her low, white form disappears over a hill or around a curve.

Long Dog is never mean to anyone. She never so much as growls. But her appearance alone will often frighten the timid, and might startle the brave who have yet to come to a belief in ghosts. People in Surgoinsville have been answering questions about Long Dog for more than 170 years. The short, sleek dog's origin is known.

In the 1820s, a thief and murderer named John Murrell plied his wicked trade on those traveling this road, before moving his operations west to Memphis and south to New Orleans. The son of an unwed brothel madam, Murrell was born in 1804. At a tender age he learned to sneak into a brothel room, while a guest was distracted by amorous pursuits, and steal what he could.

One such person the boy robbed was none other than the infamous sea pirate Harry Cranshaw, recently retired, who took an instant liking to the young Murrell. Historians have suggested that the aging pirate, one of Mom Murrell's numerous paramours, may have been the boy's father. Either way, Cranshaw happily trained the youth in the ways of crime far more wicked than the accomplishments of a small-time sneak thief. Cranshaw taught the boy the arts of murder.

Together they shot travelers from ambush and robbed the corpses, stripping the bodies of all clothing. To make sure the victims' bodies were never found, the dastardly pair developed a technique of gutting the corpse, filling it with rocks, and then dumping the whole effect into whatever water was nearby—river, creek, or swamp. Surely, the elderly Cranshaw must have been reminded of his former days of piracy when bodies were weighted and dumped overboard at sea.

Murrell emerged from youth a cruel devil of a cutthroat and nightrider who killed as he went. And he went just about everywhere. Later he would become infamous for dealing in stolen slaves and for heading a multistate organization of criminals, known as the Mystic Brotherhood, that operated throughout the South. Murrell was captured in 1834, tried in Jackson, Tennessee, and sentenced to ten years in the state penitentiary. His technique of body disposal served the villain well. No single act of murder could be proved against him, and Murrell was released from prison in 1844. In failing health, the murderous Murrell died of tuberculosis, contracted in prison, soon after his release.

There was one body, however, the maniacal Murrell failed to dispose of properly. While cavorting from crime to crime with Harry Cranshaw in his early career, Murrell was reported to have fallen upon a family of settlers camped for the night on the Old Stage Road just outside Surgoinsville, Tennessee. The family included two children. The travelers were summarily robbed of all possessions.

Once the valuables had been collected, the bandits executed the family, including the children, and stacked the bodies in the wagon. Murrell and Cranshaw hitched the horses to the family's wagon at first light and rode off to dispose of the bodies and sell the booty. But they'd forgotten something. What they forgot came running after them.

The family dog chased after the wagon as the horses pulled their inglorious cargo along the rutted road. The story has come down that Murrell took an instant liking to the idea of having a faithful dog companion, so he stopped the wagon to retrieve the friendly mutt. But this dog didn't take a liking to Murrell. She bit the bandit savagely on the arm at first opportunity and wouldn't let go.

Murrell screamed in pain, flinging the long, white dog from side to side as her teeth sank deeper into the murderer's flesh, seeking bone. Eventually Harry Cranshaw came to his associate's aid and began to strangle the dog still steadfastly attached to its human prey. Murrell writhed in brutal pain, dancing on the tips of his boot toes, while blood poured from the wound and the breath of life itself slowly seeped from the mouth of the loyal, white dog. Once the hound was unconscious, and only then, were they able to force open her mouth and free Murrell's arm.

It was an accepted belief at this time in American history that a dog bite could cause rabies, not only if the dog was carrying rabies at the time of the bite, but also if the dog ever caught rabies in the future. We know this to be mere superstition today. It was a belief, though, held firm by many well into the early twentieth century. Many family pets were put to sleep after biting someone, for fear the animal might later contract rabies and transmit the disease backwards in time to the person it had previously bitten.

No one knows if this is why Murrell killed the dog. He may have killed her out of spite. But, the white dog didn't die from Harry Cranshaw's throttling of it. She came to in the dust of the road at the bandit's feet, whereupon Murrell picked up the dog with both his powerful hands around her neck. He strangled the long, white dog until the small hound was assuredly deceased. He flung the dead animal into the roadside ditch, the only murder victim he didn't weight down and submerge in water.

Travelers on this stretch of road began seeing Long Dog not long after Murrell's raid upon the defenseless family. When wagons were the usual mode of travel, Long Dog was known to run alongside a wagon at night and jump up from time to time to peer inside. Once satisfied that whomever she was looking for wasn't present, Long Dog would stop trailing along.

Sightings of the white hound these days are usually made by the occupants of cars that have pulled over at night along Tenn. 346. Occasionally, a pedestrian walking the edge of the highway at night will enjoy the companionship of a low, white dog that keeps pace alongside and never barks. Long Dog's a dog you cannot reach out to pet. She's a ghost, an erstwhile memorial to the loyalty of the family pet.

The dog that's always wet is a ghost that appears to people indoors and has done so for a long number of years. Of unknown gender, although thought to be a male, the congenial hound inhabits several different homes in historic Greeneville, Tennessee, and as far east as Tusculum College.

Greeneville is one of the most historic communities in eastern Tennessee. It was the home of Andrew Johnson, who became the president of the United States upon the assassination of Abraham Lincoln. In 1826, Johnson moved to Greeneville, more than forty years after the community first served as the seat of government for the State of Franklin, briefly in existence from 1785 to 1788. The State of Franklin was formed as Greene, Washington, and Sullivan Counties, now in Tennessee, sought autonomy from North Carolina.

The campus of Tusculum College was designated a historic district in 1980. Construction of the oldest building on campus was begun in 1818. Another, called Old College, was built in 1841.

Numerous large homes in the area are historic, and many private residences were built before the Civil War. It is in these older houses that a large, hunting dog makes himself at home. The most recent written account, collected by Maria Auer, dates to 1962 and was printed in the *Tennessee Folklore Society Bulletin* in September 1963. A wife, who requested her last name not be taken down, and her husband James moved to the area when James got a job at a local manufacturing plant. The family rented a big house close to the college.

Folks told them the house was haunted, Myrtle said. "Well, I ain't never held with ghost stories, and the fancy tales about the house didn't bother me none, so me and Jim moved in."

The only odd thing Myrtle initially noticed was on the stairs. It seemed to her that whenever she went up or down the stairs, somebody was right behind her. But when she turned around, no one was really there. It was just a feeling, she said, nothing you could see.

Then the cat appeared. It liked sleeping in the bed she shared with James. "One night I woke up, and a black cat was in bed with me." The cat nuzzled her and purred mightily.

Myrtle remembered thinking that it was the friendliest cat she ever had. Then she woke up a little more and thought, *God, we ain't got no cat!*

"I screamed," she said, "and that cat faded into the air."

It never came back again, but the dog did—the dog that was always wet.

One of the children came in and told Myrtle there was a man and a dog in the bathtub. "Right in broad daylight," Myrtle said. The water was running because one of the children was going to take a bath. Before the child could climb in, the man and his dog appeared. They stood in the bathtub—the dog already wet as if he had been swimming.

By the time James could come to see, there was no one there. He turned off the running water. The little girl was too frightened to take a bath, so Myrtle knew something was going on. As best the little girl could describe it, it was determined the dog was a red-hair dog, probably a golden retriever. Myrtle's husband wasn't so sure there was a dog, or any other ghost for that matter, to begin with.

But James was soon convinced. He had worked a long week and was asleep on the couch in the living room that Sunday when the rest of the family was gone to church. He heard somebody at the front door and sat up. "A man walked in wearing old-fashioned clothes," Myrtle said, "a scissorstail coat and a stovepipe hat. He walked right in and didn't say nothing to Jim."

The well-dressed man walked through the room toward the back of the house. James followed him.

The man walked to the bathroom, Myrtle reported. "He walked straight to the bathroom, stepped in the bathtub and disappeared." He was looking for his dog, the dog that was always wet.

The dog has been seen in other area homes, as well. But he is never seen outside the bathtub. He appears with a human companion at times. Other times, the dog is alone. Those who are familiar with the dog's appearances believe he is the ghost of a dog that used to hunt in the area, a retriever fond of water. A golden retriever will jump in a creek after anything and is as good a swimmer as they come. Because the entire area was his to roam when the dog was alive, his ghost isn't tied to one house.

There's more than one bed-and-breakfast in the Greeneville area, especially on the east side toward Tusculum College, created from big, old handsome houses. Visitors would do well not to leave the bath running while they step outside the room to undress or retrieve articles from their suitcases.

In this specific area of eastern Tennessee, a ghost dog may get to your bath before you do. And he may bring his own company. Unlike Sticky Dog, the dog that's always wet has never been known to harm anyone.

He may show up late, with or without his hunting friend, once your bath is already begun. You'll do fine upon meeting the dog that's always wet, as long as you aren't troubled by a few long hairs wrapped around your toe nearest the drain, as long as you aren't fearful of surprises when your eyes are closed in the shower. When you drop the washcloth, or drop the soap into water, it may be the paw of a standing dog that you accidentally grab in your reaching hand. Please don't scream. Screaming bothers the neighbors.

Massengale's Gun
and The Bride Deer

*H*enry Massengale was an early settler in Tennessee. He lived in the area of the Cumberland Plateau that today is maintained as the Big South Fork National River and Recreation Area. Henry put meat on the family table by hunting along the narrow ridges and gorges of the Big South Fork River. It is an area of dramatic landscapes with high cliffs, rock arches, whitewater rapids, and plenty of edible critters.

Henry Massengale was eighty years old in the 1890s when he told his stories of a hunter's life to William Howard, a traveling sewing machine salesman. Massengale's story of a bewitched gun was originally recorded in a July 1900 issue of *The Journal of American Folklore*, accompanied by the remarkable story of a mysterious white deer that is believed to exist to this day within the deeper reaches of the neighboring Appalachian Mountains.

It was a hard winter coming when Henry's gun stopped shooting straight. His father had died the spring before. Henry inherited his father's homespun hunting shirt. It was of a heavy weave and dyed scarlet because when a deer sees red, it will stand and gaze. The shirt still worked well. Henry didn't have any trouble finding deer. He just couldn't shoot any, no matter how still a deer held for the shot.

A highly skilled and experienced hunter, Henry walked the forest silent footed, stalking his prey in moccasins even in winter. Armed with a long knife and a hatchet tucked behind a stout leather belt, he carried his trusty gun into the woods every morning and evening. And he shot nothing.

"For many years," Henry said, "I made my living hunting deer, bear, turkeys, and all sorts of varmints to be found in these mountains. I was considered a powerful good shot with a rifle, and that I certainly was." Henry provided food to other families in the area as well as his own.

"One morning, I went out and the first thing I knew I had a fine shot at a big deer, which was standing stock-still, broadside toward me." The buck stared at Henry's red shirt.

"I raised my gun, took good aim, and expected, of course, to drop him in his tracks. But I missed him point blank."

The deer bounded away. Henry followed him. The deer stood still again, "until I had wasted three shots on him and hadn't cut a hair. Then he ran off for good."

This sort of thing went on for several days, Henry said. "I had lots of powerful fine close shots, but couldn't hit a thing. I told my wife that there was something awful wrong, either with me or with the gun."

If there was a cure, Henry needed it.

He thought back on the year, wondering what could be the source of the matter.

"It's that old man's live-with," Henry's wife told him, "that old man you worked for last spring. His live-with stole everybody's bees when the apple trees were in blossom. Whole hives of honeybees flew away, queens and all, and took up at their place."

The old man's wife was a witch. Henry knew it. There were a lot of witches in the wild woods when the country was young.

"The witches turned me into a horse once I'd fall asleep at night, and they'd ride me off to their frolics," Henry said. He could distinctly recall looking at himself and thinking with swollen pride what a fine horse he was. But it was tiring, and he woke up exhausted in the morning.

On one of these occasions, the witches rode Henry through the briers, and the next morning his hands were full of thorns. His arms and legs and face were covered with red scratches.

That old man's wife was one of those witches, for sure. She never smiled at him. And she got butter out of her churn without putting in milk. She was the one that was after him, Henry decided. He knew what to do to fix his gun once he knew who had cast a spell on it.

"I went into the woods near their house, picked out a tree, and named it after the woman who lived there. After I named the tree, I shot at it and listened to see if there was any noise made at the house."

He heard something. "At the first crack of the gun I heard the woman cry out as if she had been hit instead of the tree," Henry said. "I went to the tree and found that I had hit it square on."

Henry saw the smoke rise perfectly straight up from the chimney of the house, as if it were a rope weighted on one end with a rock. Smoke only does that when the person inside a cabin is fiercely mad.

"From that time on my gun was as good as ever."

Even with his gun fixed, there was a deer in another part of the Tennessee woods that Henry Massengale would never have been able to hit. No hunter has been able to bring down the white deer of the French Broad River in Cocke County. Elijah J. Moore couldn't.

Elijah was a skilled hunter and a splendidly good shot. Hunting in the area of the French Broad River between Wolf Creek and Laurel Branch, he found a spot where the river widened into a quiet natural pool before it took up tumbling over boulders again at the next bend. He noticed a variety of recent wildlife tracks along the river's edge. Elijah tramped further back into the woods than usual, keeping an eye out for animal trails and any herbs he might see worth the picking.

A twig snapped ahead of him. Elijah looked up from the mossy shadows of the forest floor to see that he had come upon a large white deer. The deer was perfectly white, like snow. At first Elijah thought he was imagining things. The animal looked at Elijah once and then ignored him, pawing the autumn leaves with its forehooves as it searched for food.

The deer was the most beautiful animal Elijah had ever seen. Looking at the deer, Elijah felt as if his eyes had been rubbed with pearls and he was seeing into heaven.

The hunter spit into his left hand for luck, then took up his loaded long bore in both hands. He drew bead on the beast. The magnificent creature just stood there in front of him, waiting to be shot. Elijah pulled the trigger in a steady movement, letting the powder fire, holding the heavy weapon hard against his shoulder. He shot the big deer.

Well, it's probably more truthful to say that he shot *at* the deer. Elijah missed.

The hunter doesn't know how it happened—if the ball of hot lead bounced or curved—but the bullet came right back at him and hit Elijah in the leg. Upon suffering the impact, he cried out and fell to the forest floor. He had a very difficult time dragging himself home on his wounded leg.

"I don't blame the deer," Elijah said. "It was my fault for shooting at it."

He later described the deer as being incredibly beautiful. Elijah said it was as pretty as a bride in a shimmering satin dress. He also said he was relatively certain the deer had blue eyes. The magical white deer has been known as The Bride Deer ever since.

Elijah gave up hunting. So have others who have seen the Bride Deer of the French Broad River. Once his leg healed, he took up fishing on the river and, according to all accounts, became good as a bear at it. There are infrequent reports from travelers who see a large white animal from their cars on U.S. 25/70, east of Newport, where the highway follows the French Broad River through the Cherokee National Forest. The animal, if it is an animal and not a ghost, is usually seen very early in the morning or just after dusk.

Diamond Eyes

*I*t's said that more Mason jars have been sold in Newport, Tennessee, than at any other location in the world. They weren't being used to put up tomatoes. That was done at the Stokely Brothers plant, first appearing in Newport in 1905, and they used tin cans. Mason jars were popular for another reason. They were used to hold and transport moonshine.

Homemade corn liquor, moonshine, was distilled in hidden mountain coves under a cloak of secrecy and often under the cover of darkness. Any night the moon was shining was a good night for making whiskey in the hills. With autumn coming on, moonshiners were putting their final batches through the still. Distilling whiskey was a warm-weather occupation in the southern mountains.

The exception was a clandestine year-round operation in the vicinity of Piney Mountain, Rocky Top, and Beetree Knob, southeast of Newport.

There was a country church in the same area. It was built on a pleasant flat of land next to a stream and had a large stone fireplace built into the wall. One year the little log church captured the attention of a young circuit preacher named Oakley Davis. He decided to hold a revival at the church, with spirited preaching every Sunday for six weeks, to be concluded with a protracted meeting at Thanksgiving.

Word was passed among the cabins and homesteads. The first Sunday, many of the wives showed up without their husbands. Oakley Davis demonstrated an abundance of energy in his exhortation of the women to bring their men to church the next Sunday, lest the men of their families be met with eternal damnation. When Sunday came again, even fewer men were in attendance.

The preacher understood that much truth could be found in gossip. It was the lore of the women, a wealth of current information beyond the how-much-ofs and why-tos of pie and soup recipes. After Sunday supper at the house where he was staying for the week, Davis offered to help with the dishes, and while drying the plates asked the lady of the house what she believed was keeping the men from attending Sunday meeting.

"It's a ghost," she said. "The one they call Diamond Eyes. He's been out late at night by that burying yard up the hill a might. The one right next to the only path around the laurel thickets."

"I'm not sure I believe in ghosts," the good reverend said. "But if I did, I don't see how a ghost could keep a man from going to church."

"This one can see in the dark for one thing," the preacher was told. "His eyes shine like a cat, and it puts a good scare into a person at night to see those bright and shining eyes."

"I could see how a fellow would want to avoid a ghost, but I don't understand how it keeps the men from coming to meeting, I must say."

"The other part, preacher, is that the burial ground is on the trail to Wilson's still. It's the only one cooking this time of year, and Saturday night is the night a thirsty man might be walking up that way were he so inclined, him and his friends."

She went on to explain that the men traipsed up to the still on a Saturday evening as each felt the need, individually, but they usually came down as a group, some with their thirsts more thoroughly quenched than others. Diamond Eyes always showed up on the way back, standing like a tall stump at that graveyard.

The men got to where they would turn and head back to the still. They'd sit around spinning tales till morning, then come down the laurel path ghost free. Of course, they were awfully tired by daylight and many of them took to bed for their missed sleep rather than going to Sunday meeting.

"I'll put an end to that ghost," the preacher vowed. "You tell everybody about it. This Saturday night, the men should come on down the hill path at the regular time. I'll put an end to Diamond Eyes then and there. Next, I'll save their souls for their mothers and grandmothers already in heaven."

It was a good plan. The young preacher spent the week hiding in a corner of a local barn, where he prepared an elaborate headdress of candle wax and turkey feathers. It would outdo any pair of shining eyes that might be seen in the woods at night.

Oakley would beat them at their own game. They'd made up the ghost, he believed, as an excuse to keep drinking. He invented a better one. He sneaked up to the little burial plot where he hid his outfit behind the only tall headstone at the spot.

Saturday night, after most of the men had found their way to the hidden still at the high end of the mountain cove, Oakley slipped away with a white sheet under his arm. He carried an ember in a pan to the location where he would wait for the men to come down the mountain, his costume at the ready. He kept fire to a few twigs in the pan so he could light his candles when the time was right.

By the time he heard the men coming along the path, the pan was nearly full of red, glowing embers. He struggled to get his headdress in place. It was seven tiers of turkey feathers tied fast with cotton string and wax.

Oakley tied the sheet around his neck in a fashion so it entirely covered him from neck to ground. He'd show these superstitious fools a thing or two. He'd show them a ghost twice as scary as a pair of eyes that shine in the dark. Then he'd throw off his costume before the men could run. The preacher would be quick to invite them to the Lord's business on Sunday morning. They'd forget all about this ghost they made up called Diamond Eyes.

The preacher lit his candles, one in each hand. He held them out in front of him at eye level. They served the purpose of being his shining ghost eyes in the dark night. When Oakley held them right, they also illuminated his eerie headdress at the same time. He was a taller, whiter, scarier ghost than Diamond Eyes. On top of which, he could take to howling any time he felt like it.

The men saw him just fine. They stopped as a group in the middle of the trail and could not speak for a moment or two, they were so shocked by the sight.

Oakley moaned out loud. "Oh, oh, oh," he said. "Oh oh!"

"Lord a'mercy," one of the men shouted as loud as he could with a big catch of fear in his chest. He pointed right at Oakley. "Lord a'mercy! There's two of them tonight!"

Oakley turned around to see what was behind him, twirling his sheet with him. It tripped him up a bit, and he put his right foot into the pan of burning embers. A pair of sparkling ghost eyes, taller than Oakley, stared into his own. He was knee to knee with Diamond Eyes.

Then the preacher let out a scream of his own.

The men could plainly see the preacher ghost and Diamond Eyes at the same time. They could either jump into the laurel or turn around and run. They weren't as sober as they might be at other times and three of them fell, trying to turn around. The rest were most of the way back to the still when Oakley brought his candles too close to his face in an effort to keep Diamond Eyes from bearing in on him.

The turkey-feather headdress caught fire at about the same moment the bottom hem of his sheet did. The headdress roared into an instant ball of flame that lit up the entire area along with burning off all of the preacher's hair. A few seconds later, his shoe leather ignited.

Oakley whooped and hollered to high heaven, dancing into the road, the sheet finally coming free and burning in a lump at his feet. But he couldn't shake the pan from his foot.

"It's me," he screamed. "Preacher Oakley. And my foot's on fire! Help me! Help me fast!"

Two of the drunks in the trail had managed to stand up but fell over again in fits of laughter. The third picked up a broken-off branch at the side of the path and ran at the dancing preacher with it in his hand. Some of the men who had run away were returning.

"Ow-alla-aaaargh!" Oakley screamed. His foot was burned to the dickens.

The man with the branch took a swing at the young preacher's pan-fitted foot and hit Oakley's ankle instead, cracking it.

"Ow! Oh-ow-oh! Oh-ow-aaargh!"

The man took another swing with the pine branch. This time he hit the pan square, knocking it free from the preacher's foot. Red embers flew through the darkness in a shower of light.

"What's that?" one of the returning men asked another who was just ahead of him on the trail.

"Brother Davis has caught the Holy Ghost, and Bill Banner is beating it out of him with a stick. He's done knocked the preacher bald."

Oakley kicked off his shoe in no time and ran down the laurel trail lickety split. He stuck his foot into the first creek he came upon, but didn't linger.

The revival meetings ended short of their original plan. People in the area of Piney Mountain, Rocky Top, and Beetree Knob never saw Oakley Davis after that night. But they did talk about him for the longest time. Diamond Eyes, if you believe what the locals tell you, is likely to show up in the woods anytime. When he does, you may as well sit down and drink a spell. Nothing known of can scare that ghost away.

The Weeping Mausoleum

A marble mausoleum that weeps blood-red tears is one of the best-known ghost stories in Tennessee. The site of the ghost story, the Craigmiles family mausoleum in downtown Cleveland, the seat of Bradley County, is prominent and easily visited.

In the 1920s, when Katharine Trewhitt was a student at the old Central Grammar School, she recalls that as many as thirty students at a time would visit the mausoleum in October during their lunch period. The mausoleum is an impressive stone structure in the gothic style, with a steeply pitched multi-gabled roof, a dozen stone spires, and a central tower as tall as a three-story building. Polished marble columns guard the door. The building, located in the yard of St. Luke's Episcopal Church, was built more than 120 years ago of marble stone imported from Carrara, Italy.

Inside the mausoleum are six shelves and a central stone sarcophagus sculpted by Fabia Cotte, a famous Italian artist. Inside the sarcophagus rests the body of Nina Craigmiles. The remains of deceased family members occupy four of the surrounding catacombs.

Katharine Trewhitt's schoolmates in the 1920s believed, if they walked a circle around the mausoleum seven times and then approached the entrance, the door would fly open. The door's coming open to invite them in seemed especially likely in October, between the eighteenth, in particular, and Halloween.

Mrs. Trewhitt, an active member of St. Luke's Episcopal Church, conducted tours of the church and the mausoleum until very recently. She was a young and vibrant eighty-five years old as this book was going to press. She reported that, while many students circled the mausoleum seven times, no classmate she can recall was ever brave enough to walk up to the door afterwards.

It was at about this time that red stains like trails of tears appeared on the outside of the white marble walls of the mausoleum. They remain today and cannot be washed away. The red tears are welded into the stones themselves. Some people believe the tears are those of Nina Craigmiles.

Seven-year-old Nina found herself the only child of a wealthy couple in 1871 when she asked her parents if she could go to school. Her father, John Craigmiles, wouldn't hear of it. Expensive tutors came into the Craigmiles home to provide Nina with a far finer education than could ever be had by attending a public school. Because of this, Nina was without playmates.

She wanted to have other children to a party at her house on her birthday. Nina was told her birthday was too important a date not to spend it with her family. Her uncles brought her gifts. Her grandfather promised to take her for a buggy ride.

Nina was unhappy. She ignored her birthday gifts. She ate little and never smiled at her parents. Finally, her father gave in and said they would host a Halloween apple-ducking party at their home and that invitations would be sent to the families of twelve Cleveland girls her own age. The seven-year-old was pleased. Having a party wasn't as good as getting to go to school, but it was a start. She could ask other girls about school, and they would tell her everything.

Thirteen days before the big party, Dr. Gideon Thompson, Nina's grandfather, came by the house to give Nina the ride in his new buggy he'd promised her. Nina's mother, Adelia, wanted to go along.

"I think I should, Father," Adelia said.

"Not today. Nina and her old granddad can handle this rig on their own."

Nina's mother helped her into the sleek, black buggy, the top pulled up against the chill of autumn weather. There in the seat was a fine china doll dressed in lace.

"Is it mine?" Nina asked.

"You'll have to ask her yourself," Dr. Thompson said. "Her name is Camellia." The doll had the same color of hair and eyes as Nina's.

Nina took the doll into her arms and plopped onto the cushioned seat of her grandfather's new buggy. "Hello, Camellia!" Nina said. "Will you be my friend?"

"Of course, she will," Dr. Thompson said. He had the buggy hitched to his finest horse. The buggy rolled away. Nina's mother turned and walked slowly back to the house. She couldn't shake the feeling that something was wrong. A little later, when she heard the train whistle blow, her heart stopped beating. A shock went through her body. Adelia didn't know why.

Dr. Thompson wasn't paying attention to anything but making his granddaughter happy. Nina's grandfather had heard train whistles day in and day out year after year, but he'd probably never heard one quite this close before. The train coming through Cleveland on October 18, 1871, smashed into his buggy, killing Nina instantly. A porcelain doll named Camellia was broken into tiny pieces.

Nina's grandfather was thrown from the buggy on impact and, miraculously, survived the collision. He would have just as soon have died in the wreck.

St. Luke's Episcopal Church takes up an entire block of downtown Cleveland. Like the Craigmiles mausoleum, the church was constructed in a gothic style and at the family's expense as a tribute to Nina. It is built predominantly of red brick and was completed in 1874. Donated by the Craigmiles, the church was consecrated on October 18, the three-year anniversary of Nina's tragic death.

Adelia Craigmiles, widowed twice, was still alive in the 1920s. She visited Nina's mausoleum often. She would stand in the shade of the trees and remember a better time. Adelia watched the children from the nearby grammar school come to the churchyard on their lunch hour to play.

She wished Nina could play with them. She wished it with all her heart.

Nina Craigmiles must have wished it, too. It was children among these visiting grade-school students who first noticed the mausoleum was weeping. Many are convinced that the blood-red tears belong to Nina, silently crying from beyond death for the company of playmates she never knew in life.

Rattlesnake Rock

South of Laurel Bloomery, a few miles east of Mountain City, along the rugged face of the Stone Mountains, there is an easily found outcropping of flat rock known locally as Rattlesnake Rock. It's a cliffside rock that overhangs a tree-lined trail and affords any who find it a beautiful view of the mountain valleys below.

The rock is a fine place to sit and ponder life's endless possibilities— as long as you keep an eye out for nature's most unwanted visitor. On cool days, or about any day as it gets toward evening, rattlesnakes like to slither out on flat rocks to get their bellies warm. This is especially true of rocks like this one, rocks that catch the afternoon sun.

There's an old step-path that leads right to the rock. These days, the trail is likely to be overgrown with moss, and weeds, and the roots of nearby trees. When you find the rock and stand on it, you're likely to hear two things. One thing you'll hear instantly is the sound of timber rattlers underneath the rock, shaking their rattles at you for having stepped on the roof of their house.

The other thing you're likely to hear is someone playing a violin. It will sound distant at first, like wind through the green leaves at the very tiptop of the tallest trees. If you walk away quietly, very quietly, the music will follow you, people say. No one knows whether the music is from heaven or history.

As for the history possibility, there lived a man in Johnson County, along in the 1850s, who played the fiddle better than any before or since. His name was Martin.

No one in Mountain City or Shady Valley remembered ever seeing Martin without his fiddle in one hand or the other. Of course, it wasn't Mountain City in those days. The town was known as Taylorsville during the years Martin lived in the area.

Martin had a fondness for the Stone Mountains. He liked to go up there and find a fine, flat rock upon which to park his bones. He'd stay there all day and play his fiddle. When his right hand got tired of sawing the bow across the strings, he switched the fiddle neck into his other hand and would weave the bow with his left. Martin was as fine a musician with one hand on the bow as he was with the other.

The summer after he was born, Martin's mother discovered a tick on her baby boy. It was the first tick that had found its way to him, and she knew the importance of this. How the first-found tick was killed determined a mountain baby's future.

When the tick was killed upon the edge of an axe blade or hatchet, it was the baby's fate to become a skilled woodsman. When the tick's fattened body was squished upon a saw blade, the infant would grow into a fine carpenter. A woman with a beautiful singing voice was known to have a mother who killed her baby's first-found tick by smashing it on the ringing edge of a bell.

Martin's momma loved music. While her husband could tap heel-and-toe fairly well on a plank floor, and she could clap along with her hands or with a spoon against her thigh, nobody in her family played a real musical instrument. Not a mandolin, or banjo, or guitar. Not a squeezebox or fife. Not anything.

So when she found that tick, she was careful with it. She removed it with all its legs and wrapped the blood-eating bug in a small piece of cloth. With her baby under one arm and that tick cupped in her hand, Martin's momma climbed on the mule and rode eleven miles to a fiddler's cabin, where she squished that tick upon the bowstring of her neighbor's fiddle and left a little blood to dry there. The fiddler's wife was happy to let her. Martin's mother said her thank-yous and rode back home. All the way she hummed a tune she wanted her son to play when he was older.

He did.

Boy, did he. Fiddle contests were common in the mountain communities. Martin won every one he ever entered. He was most wonderfully talented and knew a thousand songs by heart by the time he was twenty. Martin didn't play a fiddle the way they do in orchestras, with the instrument tucked up under the chin and the fingertips on the bare tip-end of the bow. Martin placed the fiddle snug against the middle of his chest.

He said he played the fiddle this way so he could bob his head along with the music and not have to look down his nose all the time. Martin didn't always grab the bow by its end either. For fast dance songs, he'd pick the bow up in the middle and play a tune, with either hand, that would take the feet out from under any dancer who tried to keep up with him.

Martin could fiddle up worms when it was time to go fishing. He'd lay down in the grass alongside a nice shady spot and place the chin-end of his fiddle on the ground and play a song he'd made up himself called *Let's Go Fishin'*. The worms were all for it. They'd climb up out of the earth to see who might be playing that song. There was more than one farmer in Shady Valley who paid Martin to play a tune to get their crops to come up through the ground in spring.

They say he could stand in the deep woods and fiddle a song that would call a honeybee right to him. In Martin's day, there was a person in any county who could follow bees by sight. It was the way they found wild honey. Once Martin called the bees to his music, it was easy for the bee follower to track the bee back to its hive. For his role, Martin was given his share and always had plenty of honey.

No single girl in Johnson County was happy to be married until Martin agreed to play at the wedding.

Martin liked playing music better than he liked people. Everyone knew this and never bothered him much about it. Martin spent most of his own time up in the Stone Mountains, on that high, flat rock, playing on his fiddle from dusk to dawn. At certain times, the breeze would carry his music far across the countryside. People working in their fields miles and miles away would catch little snatches of fiddle music upon the wind. They'd smile just a little and be a wee bit happier than before. They knew it was Martin up on that big rock.

Eventually, they learned that he wasn't alone up there.

Some people who have heard a rattlesnake sound its rattle in the woods say it sounds like a fast wind through dry autumn leaves. The rattle is a series of little sounds being made so fast that the sound is a blur. That's how fast Martin could play the notes on his fiddle when he wanted to. As fast as the sound of S.

No one could play faster than Martin. Not angels. Not the devil. No one could play faster than Martin and still get the notes out. It charmed the snakes themselves, he played so well. It was his favorite thing to do—to go up on that rock and play the rattlesnakes out from hiding. The snakes couldn't find time to use their fangs, they were so charmed by Martin's music.

Boys, from time to time, followed him and they saw it happen. They came back with the same story.

"There were two dozen big timber rattlers on that rock with Martin," a boy told the first person he saw in town. "He was playing his fiddle and every one of those snakes was shaking its rattles at him and weaving its scaly head in the air, like they were all dancing."

Soon after they came back from the Stone Mountains, the boys were punished and told to stay away from that big, flat rock when Martin was playing his fiddle. A boy didn't have to be told twice. Somewhere very near that rock was a rattlesnake den.

The rattlesnakes that live in the area of the Stone Mountains are timber rattlers. What makes a timber rattlesnake different from other rattlesnakes is its propensity to inhabit a den with numerous other timber rattlers. This particular breed of rattlesnake greatly enjoys the mass communion and slithering companionship of its own kin. It is a very dangerous snake all alone, and you certainly want to avoid being bitten by one of these venomous creatures. Being bitten by ten rattlesnakes is ten times the sorrow. And that's exactly why timber rattlers are so frightening.

Martin had charmed the Stone Mountains rattlesnakes. Everyone in Mountain City and Shady Valley knew it was true. Even folks in Willen

Gap and Osborn, and over in Parker, North Carolina, believed it too. If anyone could charm rattlesnakes, it was Martin.

One old-timer in Mountain City said he knew how Martin had done it.

"He killed the biggest snake he found," the man said. "He killed one with eighteen rattles on its tail, and then he cut the rattle off and dropped it inside his fiddle so he could play faster than any poison snake can shake its tail."

As the years went by, Martin came into town less often to play. After his momma died, he sold her place and built a little cabin up in the Stone Mountains. His sister, who was ten years his younger, moved up there with him when she got married to a man from Virginia.

Martin only came down into the valley to play when he needed money. During the final years of his life, Martin played in public but once a year. That was at the fiddle contest at the Johnson County fair. He played long enough to win, then went right back to the mountain cabin he shared with his sister and her husband. Sometimes he'd stay in town long enough to buy sugar and coffee, or maybe a pig.

People were courteous to Martin. He just didn't like being around them. This is a trait that people who live in the mountains understand. Solitude is deep water, and some people like to swim there.

That last year, Martin's last year, was a very good year for fiddle music in Johnson County, Tennessee.

Rumor spread between the mountains, between the Iron Mountains to the west and the Stone Mountains to the east, that Martin was too old and too ornery to compete in the annual Johnson County fiddle contest. There was a cash-money prize for first place. Martin, the word was passed, was laid up too sick to walk down from the mountain, too ailing of late to ride a mule into town. The best fiddlers, once they heard Martin wouldn't be there, showed up in good number.

It required two entire days of mountain music, along with a whole lot of dancing and jug passing, for the judges to reduce the number of fiddlers to four finalists. The last afternoon of the contest there were four chairs set upon a wooden stage in the middle of town. People, who had traveled from all around, gathered in the streets and on the lawns. They sat in rows in the backs of wagons. Young men climbed to the roofs of the buildings in town and perched with their legs hanging down over the eaves. Young ladies danced with each other when boys proved too shy to ask.

There were many in the crowd who missed Martin's participation in the event. Others believed they heard, between the competition tunes, a sweeter fiddle music on the breeze coming down from the Stone Mountains. One or two of the old men mumbled under their breaths that Martin was coming.

There were four straight-back chairs on the wooden stage and within an hour the judges had voted two of the chairs empty. That left two fiddlers to entertain. They took turns playing sad songs and serious songs, religious songs and rip-roaring, stamp-your-feet dancing songs. The two fiddlers played songs standing up and sitting down. They played songs that made granny women laugh, and they played songs that made bold men cry. One seemed as fine a fiddler as the other. Just as fine. The crowd applauded with great enthusiasm for each fiddler and for each song.

The judges were about to call the contest a draw and split the prize money between the two finalists when they heard the crowd go hush. There was another man on stage. Like the sudden appearance of a ghost, Martin sat in one of the previously unoccupied chairs, his fiddle placed neatly across his legs, his bow in place. The other two fiddlers stepped away after nodding their respect to him.

Martin had come to break the tie. Those who knew him knew he didn't look right. His color was off. His face was sunken and spotted. His hands were gray, and you could almost see the bones of his long fingers through the mottled skin. Martin's eyes were muddy and unfocused. They rolled around like he was dead asleep and having a big dream.

He wasn't well. Martin was awfully ill, in fact. No one was sure how he managed to get himself into that chair. But there he was. And then he played, leaving the fiddle where it lay in his lap.

In torn clothes spotted with smears of mountain clay, he played. His frail head bent over his lap, Martin played the most difficult songs a fiddler could try. He played till dark, a dozen songs or more. The other fiddlers put their instruments away.

A person couldn't walk away when Martin performed. They said when you listened to him play his fiddle you forgot who you were and where you were. They said that a human heart beat so perfectly, hearing the music, a person would lift right out of her body—just a little—and wouldn't come back down till the song was over.

When Martin was finished, the crowd knew. The whole town took up a shout. He sat there with his head slumped over his lap. People leapt to their toes and whooped and whistled and bellowed. The cheer was deafening.

Some of the crowd climbed onto the stage to greet Martin and congratulate him. You didn't need judges to know who'd won the first prize. Others wanted to thank him and shake his hand. But Martin wasn't there.

The crowd milled around on stage, others joined them, toppling over all but one of the chairs. They couldn't find him anywhere. Martin was as gone as if he hadn't been there in the first place. The judges finally said they'd have someone take the money up to his cabin in the Stone Mountains in the morning.

When two men from town showed up at her cabin door the next day, Martin's sister led them carefully along a step-path that skirted a rhododendron thicket. She led them to the cliffside rock overhanging the tree-lined trail. They climbed right up to it.

"This is where we found him," she said. "Stretched out on this rock with the rattlesnakes all around. He still had his fiddle in his hand, but not his bow."

The men backed away from the rock. Having stepped on the ledge, they heard the sound of timber snakes sounding their rattles underneath the rock. Must have been a hundred of them that lived there.

"We figure he dropped his bow, and when he went reaching for it, the snakes got him," Martin's sister said. "He was bit all over and swelled up from the poison something awful."

"I'm very sorry for your loss this morning," one of the men said. He held out the prize money to Martin's sister. "We'd like you to have this on your brother's behalf."

"That's fine and dandy," she said, taking the prize money in her hand. "But it wasn't this morning that he died. It was late afternoon. We buried Martin three days ago."

The men looked at her and then at each other to make sure they'd heard it right.

"Buried him three days ago with his fiddle, we did," she said. "And with his bow, too. My husband fished it out, with a pole he cut, from the bushes under the rock ledge. Martin called it Rattlesnake Rock and I reckon so do we from now on."

The two men from Taylorsville, which is called Mountain City now, didn't have anything more to say to Martin's sister but goodbye. The men shook their heads that they'd rather not when she offered to show them the coffin hollow where she and her husband had buried Martin. Strange thing was, they both thought they heard fiddle music coming down from the Stone Mountains as they rode their horses into town. They agreed not to tell anyone a thing about it. But word gets around.

A Ghost Who Sounds Like Rain

Some people fall asleep to the sound of rain on the roof. Not Ruth May Mapes, at least not before she heard Granny Laurel's story. In 1934, ten-year-old Ruth was brought to Sevierville to spend the summer with her aunt and uncle. They lived in a big, old house at the top of a hill on the edge of town.

Ruth liked visiting her aunt and uncle, but she missed her two older brothers and her own parents. Times were tough, and the family used the warm summer months to travel the harvest the length of the Tennessee River as crop pickers. The family could make more money when they pooled their resources. The four of them slept in a canvas tent and tried their best to work seven days a week, when it wasn't raining too hard. When summer was over, her father found work in a canning plant.

Ruth's aunt and uncle had no children of their own, and they showered the young girl with attention. They had a new doll waiting for her. The doll was dressed in clothes Ruth's aunt had made for it, from the same material and pattern she used to make Ruth's fancy Sunday dresses. They both got new shoes, too.

Ruth was allowed to sprinkle lots of brown sugar on her oatmeal in the morning. In the afternoon, she hosted tea parties on the front porch. Her tea set was china, just like a real one, and she had to be very careful with it. Her doll was guest of honor. There was honeysuckle vine on the lattice at one end of the porch, and morning glories on the other. Ruth liked it there.

For an hour on Sundays, she had to sit in the parlor with her doll and be very quiet while her aunt and uncle listened to Cousin Jody play Hawaiian guitar on the radio. Ruth curled up on the fireplace hearth and waited. It was cool on the tiles at the front of the fireplace. Afterwards, her aunt let her eat cookies on the front porch.

It rains regularly in the summer in Tennessee. It seemed to rain especially on Sundays. One Sunday when Cousin Jody was through playing talk-guitar, Ruth's uncle turned off the radio and left the women to their late afternoon. Ruth thought she might go out back and try to climb that tree. Or maybe she'd sit in the swing they put up for her and let her bare toes press prints into the soft dirt under it.

That's when she heard the rain.

"I guess I won't," she said out loud.

"Won't *what?*" her aunt asked.

"Go outside and sit in the swing," Ruth said. "It's raining."

Ruth's aunt peered out the window. "It doesn't seem to be raining any in front," she said, puzzled. The parlor was built onto the side of the two-story house. It had its own roof and the new brick fireplace.

"I can hear it on the roof." Ruth looked straight up. It was directly over her. The sound of rain.

"Come here, Ruthie May," her aunt said.

Ruth did. The sound of rain pelting the roof followed her across the room.

"Do you hear it now?" Ruth asked.

"Yes, I do," her aunt confessed. Then the sound ended. "But it isn't raining, darling. The sun's shining."

Ruth darted outside without her shoes on. She wrote the shape of a heart with her big toe in the soft dirt under the wooden swing. Then she thought about climbing the tree. If she could just get to that first big limb, the one the swing's ropes were tied to, she bet she could climb to the top of the whole thing.

That's when she heard it again. The sound of rain was in the tree overhead. As plain as day, she heard it. She smelled it, too. It smelled just like rain.

As the days wore on, it began to happen all the time. The sound of rain followed Ruth Mapes around the house. It followed her out on the porch. It sometimes showed up in the trees. About the only days she didn't hear it was when it was really raining.

At night, she heard it raining on the roof over her bed. Ruth got up. She went to the open window where the lace curtain lifted on the breeze. She peeked outside just long enough to see if it was raining or not. The shadows in the yard and in the trees turned into things and started moving around if you looked at them too long at night, if you looked at them directly.

It wasn't raining.

Ruth went right back to bed and looked up at the ceiling. "Please stop now," she said softly, like a whispered prayer. The sound of rain stopped when she asked it to. The next day, it returned.

"It follows you around like a hungry kitten," her aunt said. "Your uncle doesn't hear it, Ruthie May. He doesn't hear it at all. But I think it's time we do something about it, don't you?"

"Do what?" Ruth wanted to know.

"I think we should visit Granny Laurel from church and get to the bottom of this."

"Yes, ma'am," Ruth said. She'd likely get cookies and real tea in real china cups with real sugar cubes! "May I bring my doll?"

"Of course you may. Now put your socks and shoes on, Ruthie May, and we'll walk together to Granny Laurel's house. She'll know what this is about, if anyone does."

Ruth's aunt brought along a loaf of freshly baked bread in a wicker basket. The bread was wrapped in white linen. There were six pats of butter along for the ride. Ruth had helped make them from the wooden mold that pressed the picture of a tulip into each one.

Granny Laurel was the church historian and had worked in the county clerk's office for years. She also drew up family trees for people who lived in the area. Granny Laurel wrote a column in the paper about what people were doing, who showed up for the church suppers, and who had visitors from out of town. She knew everything about everybody in Sevierville.

They didn't have tea. Granny Laurel had a bad spell and was in bed. Her daughter was in the house to help with things and said it would be just fine if Ruth and her aunt went upstairs to talk with the older woman for a short while. She thanked them both for the bread and butter.

"It's not the first time," Granny Laurel said when Ruth's aunt asked her about the sound of rain on the roof of their house. "Does the sound follow this little darling from room to room and out on the porch, too?"

"Yes, it does," Ruth's aunt said.

"And you never heard it before?"

"That's right. It started when Ruthie May came to visit."

"He likes the little girl," Granny Laurel said. She smiled at Ruth.

"He?" Ruth's aunt asked quickly.

"Yes. And there's another girl you need to hear about," the old woman said. Granny Laurel shared the story as she had heard it.

The house Ruth's aunt and uncle lived in was built in the 1850s. A doctor lived there after the war, with his wife and daughter. Granny Laurel didn't remember the girl's name, but said she was about the same age as Ruth.

The doctor had a fine reputation throughout the area. One hot day in August a wagon pulled up to the house. An old black man, an ex-slave named Luther, climbed down from the wagon and collapsed on the spot. Fresh water was brought to him, and he was helped into the carriage house where he was given a cot upon which to rest from his journey.

Luther had driven his wagon in the heat of the sun all the way from his farm by Wear Valley. He had caught a miserable fever days before and now feared he was about to die. He felt horrible, said he saw dragons in the road, and couldn't think straight.

It was about his time to go, the doctor told Luther. A young girl standing behind the doctor started crying. The doctor didn't know his daughter had followed him to the carriage house, but there she stood, weeping her heart out at what her father had told the old man. She wouldn't stop crying until they moved Luther inside the house.

"Give him my room," the girl insisted. "It's the coolest in the house."

Her father wanted her to stay out of it, but she wouldn't hear a thing he said. The doctor dissolved a powder in a cup of water for the dying man to drink. It would make him feel better, the doctor said.

Luther was put into the girl's bed, after all, where she sat next to him and sponged cool spring water on the dying man's quivering face and forehead.

"It's so hot," the old slave said. "It's so hot, Missy, I fear I'm there already." He opened his eyes and stared straight ahead.

"Oh, I don't know," the girl said. "Maybe it will rain and that will cool you off some. It could rain any minute now." She held the sponge gently to his forehead.

"It might rain," she said again. "Any minute now."

Luther closed his eyes and died.

It rained that evening. A big thunderstorm rolled in. It rained all night and all the next day.

"It rained to beat the band," Granny Laurel said to her bedside company. "But even after the rain stopped and the storm moved away, the sound of rain could be heard on the roof of that house. It followed that doctor's daughter as she moved from room to room."

"Just like me," Ruth said.

Granny Laurel agreed. "You must remind Luther of the young girl who was his only comfort when he died. Does the sound of rain stop when you ask it to?"

"Yes, it does."

"That's Luther, then. It's just his ghost saying thank you."

Ruth's aunt thanked the woman for the story and said perhaps they should be leaving now. Granny Laurel said she was pleased to have had company and urged them both to come back when she might be feeling better. Once they were on their way home, Ruth asked her aunt if the story Granny Laurel had told them was true.

"She's the church historian, Ruthie May. She wouldn't lie to you."

The sound of gentle rain was on the porch roof later that day when Ruth came out to smell the honeysuckle. She stood stock-still and listened. She smiled. It felt just a little bit cooler to stand under the sound of rain.

Ghost Funeral at Grassy Cove

Motorists on Interstate 40, in the vicinity of Mount Roosevelt State Forest, enjoy a series of breathtakingly pretty views of the Cumberland Plateau. Along the twenty miles or so between the Tennessee River and Exit 329 at Ozone, travelers heading west pull their cars over to the shoulder on a regular basis. They park briefly to better savor the panorama of lush, rolling mountains. Some step out of their cars to take pictures.

Just south of Ozone, accessible on Tenn. 68 out of Crossville, is one of the prettiest views in the entire state. The highway descends into a gorgeous three-thousand-acre mountain valley called Grassy Cove, which is also the name of the small town there. Grassy Cove is postcard-pretty at almost any time of the year.

At the time of the Civil War, potassium nitrate was mined from the floor of one of the larger caves in the area. It was used to manufacture gunpowder for the Confederacy, a process carried out at a smaller cave a little further from town. A large spring near this cave is known to locals yet today as Powder Mill Spring.

Soon after the close of the war, a discovery in a cavern connected to the saltpeter mine put into play a series of events that resulted in a secret held in union by all the residents of the mountain valley. The discovery was that of a body that soon became known as the petrified man.

According to Stella Mowbray Harvey, in her book *Tales of the Civil War Era*, a community decree issued soon after the body's discovery forbade mention of the incident by local citizens because of the negative effect the discovery had upon the lives of the people. Mrs. Harvey refers to the decree as a chimney-corner law. "At church, Sunday School, and other public gatherings the people were exhorted to cease speaking of the petrified man at any time or place in order to quiet the minds of the people."

She went on to add, "In event this request was ignored, a stronger rule would be put into effect whereby offenders would be prosecuted by law for spreading false rumors."

It is safe to conclude that the entire valley was haunted by the disquieting effects of the petrified man. The discovery was made by boys who explored the old mine, looking for hidden treasure. The boys ventured further back through a series of connected caverns than even the miners had gone before. Instead of gold coins and family silver hidden from marauders during the Civil War, the adventuresome boys came upon the body of the petrified man.

The corpse of the man had solidified over the years through exposure to minerals in his underground tomb. The cavern may have been flooded in past seasons with limestone-enriched ground water. In any event, the body seemed to be made entirely of rock.

Men were summoned, including the coroner and the sheriff. Murder was out of the question. The body was in peaceful repose, hands folded upon the chest, without wounds or visible marks of any kind. It was as if the man, thought to be approximately thirty-five years old, had gone to sleep and, while snoozing, had been turned to stone.

It was surmised that the cause of death was natural, and that the hardening of the body took place after death. The petrified man soon became the talk of the valley. People who had lost loved ones in the war visited the slate-smooth corpse, hoping it might be the remains of a son, brother, or father yet to be found. The dead man remained unrecognized.

Eventually, a Christian burial was provided for the corpse. According to Mrs. Harvey's history of the event, Parson William Rush and Reverend Chris Ford conducted graveside services. The petrified man was buried in the graveyard alongside the Methodist Church, where on weekdays grammar school was being taught by Julius Hamby.

Many were present, including a man named Simon, a former slave from a nearby family farm. Simon was there to close the grave for his usual twenty-five-cent fee. Leaning on his old shovel, the former slave moaned through the whole ceremony. He mumbled to himself and to anyone else who would listen that something mighty was the matter.

"If a body don't want to go in the ground, you shouldn't put it there," he told the two preachers.

They didn't know what Simon meant.

"Why, didn't you see him shaking his head no the whole time you were wording over him?"

"No, I didn't." Parson Rush said. "And neither did you, Simon." The homemade coffin was kept closed during the service.

Simon threw the dirt on, mumbling the entire time it took to close the grave.

Trouble walked the valley almost immediately. As soon as it was dark, people heard voices descend from the area of the cave, voices that came through town. There were voices to be heard, but nothing to see. A horse could be ridden right through the middle of the voices, and they wouldn't go away.

And then there was the hollering. Not dog howling, but the human kind. All night long, someone hollered back and forth on the road beside the Methodist Church. Other people reported the front door of the church itself was opening and slamming shut like someone playing a drum. Bam, bam, bam.

Soon, the whole valley wasn't getting any sleep. The children refused to go to school at the Methodist Church, which was okay by Julius Hamby. The teacher moved his lessons to the Primitive Baptist for the duration of the season. Many adults could not be made to travel the road past the graveyard.

Simon figured it out first.

He took his theory to Parson Rush, who said he would think about it some. He visited Reverend Ford, who wanted to know what the parson said. Attendance at the Methodist Church was down to a precious few oldsters, who shared near-deafness as a trait.

"I'll do it for fifty cents, if no one else will," Simon said. "I'll dig him up for you. But someone else will have to do the preaching to those ghosts."

It was Simon's theory that it took such a long time for a body to turn to stone that the petrified man's only friends were from the other side of death. "They're all ghosts who know him best. They've been ghosts together for a long number of years, I figure."

Simon's was a considered opinion. "When you took that man from his resting place in that cave and buried him in the ground, you took him away from his friends. They're missing him is what's going on. You didn't invite any of them to the funeral. That funeral you had was for the living."

"So you believe they want a funeral for their friend?" Parson Rush asked.

"I believe they are demanding it," Simon said. "I'll dig him up for fifty cents, but someone else will have to do the preaching."

"Where will we put him this time?" Reverend Ford wanted to know.

"One of the caves," Simon suggested. "But I wouldn't tell anyone where. They'll take to hearing things, if they know where they're supposed to hear them."

The church bell was rung. Men from surrounding farms gathered. Simon removed the dirt from the petrified man's grave. The coffin was raised and placed on a wagon. A pact was made among the leaders of the community. All agreed. What happened next would never be mentioned.

At dark, Parson Rush climbed onto the wagon and took the reins. Lanterns were tied to the footsteps. Simon threw the shovel on, then climbed aboard and sat beside the coffin. The wagon drew slowly away, up the winding road to the niter mine.

It caused the two men some difficulty to remove the coffin and drag it into the mine, but they managed.

"Better give it one of your best," Simon advised the parson. "I'd say an hour or more is properly called for."

Simon took one of the lanterns and his shovel to a spot distant from the big cave. He had started on the secret digging earlier in the day and only had the final foot to go.

Parson Rush preached a dandy ashes-to-ashes sermon to the ghosts of Grassy Cove, gathered in the niter cave. His voice lifted, echoed off the stone walls of the underground cavern. It was like having a chorus. No one alive knew what he said.

When he came outside, Simon was sitting there.

"Thought maybe they invited you to supper," Simon said.

"I had more to say than I thought I might," Parson Rush confessed. "No one interrupted me in any way. I think it's the first time in my life I preached straight through without a single hacking cough or a baby crying. I have to hand it to them, ghosts are the best listeners I've ever found."

Simon and the parson loaded the coffin on the wagon. They buried it in the secret location. When they left, Simon walked behind the wagon for the first fifty yards, obscuring the tracks with a piece of brush.

The community returned to normal. The ghosts never came back to town. Or if they did, they did so quietly without bothering anyone. Julius Hamby moved his subscription school back to the Methodist Church and all the children came with him.

The only difference, really, was that a grave was left open alongside of the church for a couple weeks. The citizens of the community could see for themselves that the previous trouble was now removed. People who passed the graveyard were no longer pestered by anything.

In her published history, Stella Mowbray Harvey reveals the location of the original burial plot. There is a small stone vault marked with the name Floyd in the Methodist cemetery at Grassy Cove. "A third grave space to the left of the vault," Mrs. Harvey notes, "would mark the post where a grave was opened in which to bury the petrified man."

Occasionally, some wag in the community would start up a tale about the petrified man. He was quickly visited and told that prosecution to the fullest extent of the law would follow if he were to mention the incident again.

You're welcome to visit Grassy Cove today. It's peaceful and pleasant. You can even visit one of the caves (except on Sundays), if you ask permission first at the Kemmer & Sons Store on Tenn. 68. But don't expect anyone to go on at length about the petrified man. People in Grassy Cove, like people everywhere else, need their sleep.

Double-headed Hitchhiker

CARTER COUNTY

An old crime long forgotten has produced an eager hitchhiker in Carter County, Tennessee. Gap Creek Road runs south from Watauga Point, through Big Spring and Gap Creek, to Gap Run at Tenn. 361. A tall ghost lurches from roadside shadows toward any vehicle passing late at night along a particular curve of this road, wet weather or dry. The ghost is so tall, in fact, some people who have seen him think he is wearing a high hat—one of those old-time stove pipe hats.

A few people, those most easily frightened, believe instead that the ghost has two heads, one on top of the other. Cars outrun the double-headed hitchhiker from time to time. Other times, a driver is not so lucky. After the towering ghost catches a lift, he is through for the night.

And what a ride it is! Once the tall figure grabs hold of a moving car, he doesn't let go. You couldn't pry him loose with a shovel. Wherever he grabs the car—door handle, front bumper or back—he quickly climbs to the top of the car. The tips of his shoes can be seen at the top of the rear window.

The view is worse through the front windshield. Initially his hands appear, five bloody fingertips on the driver's side, then five bloody fingertips on the passenger's half. The ghost is gearing up to look inside. His hat appears, if you think it's a hat, followed by a set of peering eyes, looking straight and hard at the driver and then at whoever else is in the car. If you're one of those who believes the hitchhiker is double-headed, first a head appears, then another. One head is on top of the other, like olives on a toothpick.

Frightened drivers have swerved to throw him off the car. This is not advised. Others have slammed on the brakes. It doesn't do any good. What the double-headed (or high-hatted) ghost wants is a ride around the curve. And he wants it every night.

The blood on his hands is his own, if you believe the story of Jubal and James, brothers from down around Gap Run. James was older, but Jubal was taller. Jubal was so tall and thin that people said he resembled Abraham Lincoln.

James had a little bit of money in 1928. He worked at the sawmill and had about six acres in potatoes. James decided to use his money to get himself a wife. He was the older brother, and it was time he got married.

"I want to meet the finest woman in Carter County," James told his younger brother. "I want a real peach of girl, Jubal, a snappy piece of work. I want to marry the best there is. No pill or pickle or priss will do."

"The best," Jubal agreed, nodding. *How was his brother going to do that?*

"A peach, Jubal. A real sweet patootie."

Patootie was a word they used in the 1920s. No one laughed at that.

"I surely hope you do," Jubal said. But he didn't see how.

James knew how. He took every dime he had and bought a car. His car came on the train from Michigan. It was a Ford Model A in a nice tan color called Arabian Sand, with a self-starter and other fancy gadgetry. It had a shatterproof windshield, the first of its kind.

The car arrived just in time for the Fourth of July festival and fireworks show at Big Spring. It was the biggest of times, an outdoor picnic and party that lasted till midnight. Every peach of a girl in the county would be there.

This was a time in small-town America when people dressed up in costumes for the Fourth of July. They dressed up like patriots and presidents, like George and Martha Washington, like Uncle Sam. Ladies wore red-striped dresses with blue stars sewn on. They wore dresses with red, white, and blue sashes.

James didn't want to wear a costume. He believed he looked his best without one. Jubal, though, decided to go as Abraham Lincoln. He dressed in black. He put black shoe polish on his face in the trimmed-back fashion of Lincoln's beard. His old pappy let him wear his gold watch from the Civil War. Jubal wore it in a vest pocket with the big gold chain in a single loop on his left side.

Jubal topped off the effect with a tall stove pipe hat he rented from the undertaker in Hampton for a nickel.

"With that hat on," his pappy said, "you look seven feet tall. Be careful with my watch, you hear."

James and Jubal rode to the picnic and fireworks show in James's new Model A. The car was as pretty as any gold watch. James found exactly what he was looking for. A sweet patootie. He showed her his car. She climbed inside to try out the seats. By the time it was dark, she and James were holding hands. When the first fireworks exploded in the sky, they kissed.

Jubal, when he wasn't dodging firecrackers tossed by the younger boys, spent his time having fun with the other people in costumes. He posed with them for pictures. He held his pappy's gold watch in his right hand with the case lid open, as if he meant to check the time the play at Ford's Theatre was supposed to begin. He held it in his right hand, so people could see the heavy gold chain looped on the left side of his vest. Jubal used his left hand to tug at the narrow brim of his stove pipe hat whenever he walked close to a lady.

James found Jubal to tell him the situation.

"If I'm to get her to marry me, Jubal, I'm going to have to drive her home alone. You know it's why I got the car in the first place."

Jubal knew. He didn't want to walk home. But it was a warm night out, and there wasn't any rain. He supposed he could trudge the miles from Big Spring to Gap Run.

"I tell you what, I'll take her on home after the fireworks are over and then I'll come back up the road to find you. If you're still walking, I'll give you a lift."

"Kiss her once for me, will you?" Jubal said.

Jubal, who was watching the fireworks alone and didn't have a picnic blanket to sit on, left before the fireworks were quite finished. Other people were leaving, too. Some were in cars, others on buckboards and in wagons hitched to horses. Some walked.

As he put a little footfall between himself and the picnic, the fireworks were even prettier. You could see them better from a distance. Jubal's long legs and open stride carried him quickly ahead of the other pedestrians. They seemed to lollygag anyway, couples with their arms around each other. Jubal walked alone. Maybe someone he knew from Gap Run would come by and offer him a ride. He hiked alongside the road.

His rented stove pipe tilted from side to side as he marched at the road's edge. Jubal tugged it into place more than once, to keep it from slipping. Finally, somewhere south of where the road crossed Scaffold Branch, he pulled the tall hat down snug with both hands from either side until it wedged tightly over the top of his ears. There. It would stay put for awhile.

There seemed to be fewer and fewer people behind him. And the road itself was empty now, empty for quite a spell. Jubal knew Gap Creek Road well, and there were two big curves ahead that could be easily short-cut by walking through the corner of a field, once you jumped a ditch. Jubal elected to make up some distance by walking a couple hundred yards over land.

Someone trailing him had the same idea. He could hear them hurrying along behind him as he came to a tree on a slight rise. Jubal paused briefly, thinking to wait to say hello to the people coming along. He didn't have to wait.

It was only one man, and he was running straight at Jubal. There was something in his hand.

Jubal sucked in his breath.

"Whoa there, now!" he said. His saying it had no effect. The man smacked right into Jubal as if on purpose, knocking him down. He pushed at Jubal with one hand and prodded at Jubal with the other.

"Gimme your watch!" the stranger said. It was somebody from the picnic.

The man's breath stank of liquor, and Jubal realized too late that he was being attacked. The man meant to rob Jubal of his pappy's gold watch and chain. His assailant had a knife in one hand.

"Give it to me, or I'll stick you deep!" the robber said.

Jubal kicked at him. He cut both of his hands by trying to grab the man's knife. It stung pretty badly. They were deep cuts.

Jubal kicked again and again and scrambled about, twisting the man almost entirely off of him. Jubal felt himself be stabbed. In the chest. It hurt like he had been hit by a bullet, he thought. Jubal stood up. He still had his hat on.

He swung wildly at the stranger, connecting. He moved away but only a step or two. Jubal was stabbed in the back. It wasn't bad. The robber must have been off balance. Jubal turned and swung his fist with swift but unsure violence and luckily connected with the man's face, knocking him back. Jubal ran toward the road.

He stumbled. He fell. He got back up again. He splashed through the ditch water and pulled himself up the other side, where he stood to catch his breath. It hurt to breathe. His belly hurt, too. He patted his vest to feel for his pappy's watch. It was still there, but his hands came away soaked with blood.

Jubal lurched forward toward a pair of large headlights he saw on the road, coming from the north. He heard his assailant splash into the ditch directly behind him. Jubal stepped into the road in front of the oncoming car. He held one hand to his aching belly. He raised his other hand to hail the car to stop. It hurt something awful to reach his arm up.

He skipped a few steps along the road, away from the attacker's certain approach. The car was upon him. It was a brand-new Model A painted in the color the factory called Arabian Sand. It was James behind the wheel. And sitting next to him was the sweet patootie James had met at the picnic.

They couldn't see Jubal too well. He looked dirty or drunk. James had to swerve to keep from hitting him.

"Who's that?" the fairer passenger asked her stalwart driver.

Jubal fell to the road on his knees. He was bleeding badly.

"Don't know who that could be," James lied, thinking his brother was pulling some kind of prank. Leave it to Jubal, he thought, that boy would never grow up.

"It looked like Abraham Lincoln," the girl said, giggling. "I'm glad you didn't hit him."

The Model A left Jubal behind. And his assailant was soon upon him to finish the job. He stabbed Jubal in the heart, took the watch and chain, and rolled his body to the side of the road. Jubal's body was found by others walking the road a short time later. He was still wearing his stove pipe hat, which was returned directly to the man from whom it had been rented—the undertaker.

He was buried at age seventeen in a long casket, but Jubal was never properly put to rest. If his brother had stopped for him, instead of swerving to one side, it might have saved his life. If Jubal had grabbed secure hold of the car, he might have made it to safety.

Jubal must believe so, because he keeps trying. The tall, shadowy figure on Gap Creek Road is the ghost of a man murdered on the Fourth of July, the story goes. The ghost is that of a young man attempting to outrun his fate. He doesn't have two heads, although it may look like it. It's just a hat. Perhaps he'd like to have his pappy's gold watch back, but what he really seeks is a ride to safety around a certain curve on Gap Creek Road. He'll likely try it again tonight and tomorrow night, and every night thereafter.

James got married, but he sold the car after that night. Word in Carter County is he took a loss.

Lover Lady Bumper Jumper of Dark Hollow Road

The double-headed hitchhiker of the preceding chapter is not, re-markably, Carter County's only ghost known to jump on cars. There's the Lover Lady Bumper Jumper of Dark Hollow Road who does the same thing, just about.

Sugar Hollow Road originates at the big bend of Tenn. 143 in Roan Mountain State Park. The country road leads south out of the park. Not far beyond the community of Sugar Hollow, the road is intersected by Dark Hollow Road, which, traveling east, joins Sugar Hollow Road to Hampton Creek Road. A small cemetery sits at a point along the ap-proximately 1,500 yards of Dark Hollow Road.

For one of its occupants, the cemetery is not a quiet, restful place.

Legend has it that the ghost of a lady named Delinda is looking for a way out of the cemetery on Dark Hollow Road. When a car drives by late at night, she is known to jump onto the back bumper. She can't al-ways be seen, but she can be felt. The ghost's jumping onto the back bumper of a car gives it a little bounce.

While Delinda can rarely be seen at all clearly, her shadow is distinct.

It can be seen upon the surface of the road when illuminated by a car's taillights. A flashlight, however, shone in her direction will pass right through the ghost, illuminating nothing. One way to know for certain whether Delinda is on the bumper of a car is for the driver to come to a stop and put the vehicle into reverse. This brings on the brighter back-up lights, which better show the unwavering shadow of a woman with long, flowing hair.

A driver who, for whatever reason, parks a car in the vicinity of the cemetery at night is likely to feel the jolt of someone jumping onto the rear bumper. There, standing on the bumper of a parked car or pickup, the ghost will wait patiently for a ride away from the scene.

According to the whispered tales that high school students in the area share with each other, the ghost isn't looking for a ride. They say Delinda is looking for love. And she well may be. Delinda is also known as the Lover Lady of Dark Hollow Road.

You won't find a tombstone in the cemetery with her name on it. There's a reason for that. It's also the reason Delinda's ghost cannot find rest. When she died, Delinda was not allowed a proper, church burial. How she died is a bit of a mystery. Why she died is not. If she didn't die for love, she certainly died because of it. You might say Delinda loved too much.

Delinda had silky black hair and pale-white skin. She lived alone in a one-room cabin at the top of a steep hill. Delinda had a boyish figure. But form didn't keep her from being pleasing to men. In life, Delinda was quite the lover. She loved many men in the area, married men for the most part.

They loved her back. And they loved her often. The men brought her gifts when they visited, baubles and candy, ribbons and perfume. Sometimes they brought her silver coins for her collection, which she kept in a jar behind a loose rock in the wall of the fireplace. They also brought her food—fresh eggs and milk, jars of apple butter and preserves, ham. Married men spent their money and time on Delinda when they should have been spending it at home.

Delinda got sick one summer. She caught the flu, or something like it. It wasn't long until most of the men, the married men who were loving Delinda as frequently as they could afford, came down with the same ailment. It hurt when they coughed. The sickness sapped them of their strength, and very few of them could work. This upset their wives.

It also upset the circuit preacher. There were no men in church, except for a few young boys and an older gent. The husbands were at home sick.

The preacher told the women they should put a stop to what was going on. He didn't tell them to run Delinda out of town, but that's what they set out to do. A visiting committee was formed. Eden Jankins, a devout churchgoer, was elected president of the committee, and the local ladies, toting their husbands' squirrel guns, marched in a group to Delinda's house at just after dark. A couple of old hounds tagged along, thinking the ladies were after possum or raccoon.

That was the last anyone saw of Delinda. Alive.

A strange coincidence occurred. A Mr. Jankins was killed later, on that same date, in a tragic hunting accident. Though sick in bed, he was cleaning his squirrel rifle after his wife Eden was through with it. She must have left it loaded by mistake, because right smack in the middle of the night, Mr. Jankins shot himself in the chest with it.

As sad as it was that he had a hole through one lung and maybe a corner of his heart, Mr. Jankins looked peaceful in death. Everyone who saw him laid out in the front room of the house said he looked just as if he were fast sleep in a warm, soft bed.

The preacher was sent for. It would be tomorrow before he could hurry back to the church to preach the funeral.

Eden's oldest son built a box out of fourteen-inch barn wood, and they carried Mr. Jankins down to the church in it. Eden Jankins followed along. The boys carried shovels and a pick to the small cemetery to open the ground in anticipation of Mr. Jankins's arrival. They worked all night.

Eden Jankins stayed at the church, stayed with her husband in his box. One by one, ladies from the visiting committee showed up to keep her company in her despair. One brought with her a hammer, and a handful of square-headed nails, in a cloth sack. Another brought a small bottle of precious perfume to daub onto a lady's handkerchief when the smell of death overcame the small church.

Someone passing said he saw one of the women lying down on the ground in grief, just alongside the church door. The other women were gathered around, pulling at her, trying to help her up. He didn't know if it was Eden Jankins. But it must not have been, he told the boys at the gravesite, because the woman on the ground had long black hair. Mrs. Jankins's hair was blonde.

"It's night, can you be sure her hair was black?" Eden's oldest son asked. He was worried after his mother's health.

"Pretty sure, though it was shadowy there by the church steps," the neighbor said. "Of course, the door was open and a miser's share of light tumbled out. I could see your father's open coffin there in the church from where I walked."

The women of the visiting committee, the women who arrived with perfume and nails to sit with Eden Jankins in her grief, had the door of the church closed tight when the neighbor passed by on his way home that night. He started toward the church, to see if there were something he might do. The thought of a group of helpless, wailing women, their faces wet and red and wrinkled with tears, put him off the idea, and he kept walking.

It was just a little after that, he heard hammering from somewhere behind him. Somebody was repairing a wagon seat, he thought, or a chair. He had one of each at home that needed attention. He kept walking.

Those who weren't too sick with the flu, or something like it, gathered for the funeral about noon. The women had a table set with food outside the church, in the shade of tall trees there. They had their handkerchiefs daubed once with perfume. The smell inside was strong enough to need two daubs.

To everyone's surprise, the barn-wood coffin was nailed shut. Nailing a dead person in before he was preached over wasn't the usual way. The ladies of the visiting committee explained to those who complained that the widow couldn't bear to see her poor husband dead one minute more.

"No one should say another word about it," one of the ladies of the visiting committee said. She was Eden's closest friend. "Not another word."

They paid the preacher with twenty shiny dimes from a collection the women of the visiting committee had taken up. He spoke at length on how it was a man's duty to surrender all to God. He noted that Mr. Jankins had done that.

The four Jankins boys, three sons and one cousin, were duty bound by blood to carry the casket to the flatbed wagon at the front of the church. A gentle horse waited in the harness for the slow walk to the cemetery.

One of the boys must have picked up a splinter in his palm. He dropped his end of the deep-sided box. Eden Jankins gasped. The other three boys acted quickly to ease the casket down at a steep angle to keep from upending it. The preacher lay his Bible aside and stepped forward to assist. He was a big man, and he took up the whole tail end of the homemade coffin, while the boys carried it from the front and sides.

The preacher didn't recall the deceased having been such a heavy man. Still, he figured Mr. Jankins's weight wouldn't keep him from being lifted to heaven. Other things might. At the cemetery, the preacher helped the boys move the box to the edge of the open grave. They set it down on ropes arranged for the purpose and carefully lowered the box into the hole.

The hole was deeper than some graves.

"Ashes to ashes," the preacher said. "Dust to dust."

The widow dropped in a small handful of dirt.

"Amen."

Some people had expected Delinda to show up at the funeral. She was watched for.

It was just after Mr. Jankins's funeral that everyone along Dark Hollow way noticed that Delinda seemed gone for good. A young man, his wife, and his three children moved into her old cabin. They'd been living with the old folks and needed a place.

People talked about Delinda like she might have been a witch. There were stories about strands of her long black hair found here and there throughout the region, turning up in the butter. None of that was true.

Whether or not the Lover Lady of Dark Hollow Road was at the funeral is another case altogether more difficult to conclude. Some say no. Some say so.

Some say she was there alright, but that Delinda was lying down.

They say she was lying down in that barn-wood box, lying down in death, as she had in life, check-to-cheek with a married man.

For the concern of history, there's no record of the Lady Lover Bumper Jumper being buried in the cemetery off Dark Hollow Road. There's no headstone with her name on it. If she's at the bottom of a grave in a box with another corpse, the bones of their limbs intertwined, Delinda must be unhappy with the arrangement. Her ghost keeps looking for a ride the heck out of there. Or maybe Delinda jumps on the bumpers of cars just to give the boys who are driving a little bounce.

Rumor has it if you get out of your car and stand in the cemetery off Dark Hollow Road at night and if, at the exact moment of midnight, you toss a shiny dime high into the air overhead, it never lands. Something or someone grabs hold of it before it can hit the graveyard grass.

Cold Night, Warm Girl

Gatlinburg, Tennessee, is one of those places in America where people go to be wed. It is estimated that more than ten thousand couples are married annually in Gatlinburg. Honeymoon chalets are tucked in along both sides of the narrow valley that runs through town. Gatlinburg is also at the edge of the lush, steep inclines into the Great Smoky Mountains National Park. The town has long been a gathering place for pure-bred mountain folk who come down out of the mountains to trade hand-made crafts.

It wasn't always the case that young men looking for a girl to spark first bought themselves a car.

In the autumn of 1910, a young man named Foster rode his big roan horse down the rugged trail from Piney Mountain way to a little church at the edge of Gatlinburg. The Methodists were having a protracted meeting. Foster went to church somewhere every week and for all the right reasons. He was looking for a wife.

Church was the proper place to find the marrying kind, his mother told him. The old Cherokee woman who lived near Foster, at the other end of the hollow, told him the same thing. He'd learned over the years to take her advice just about any time she cared to give it. The old lady knew things.

The Cherokee woman was close to nature, as Foster's mother liked to put it. She always knew, for instance, when it was going to rain and when it was going to stop. She knew what to do when the cow quit giving milk or the churn wouldn't make butter. Foster asked the old lady about almost any problem he came across, including this recent one of finding a wife.

"Go to church," she said, agreeing with his mother. "Go to church, Foster, and you'll do just fine."

Foster thought it would be easier if he scrambled to the top of Mount LeConte and hollered for a wife. He'd heard that's what the men in Switzerland did. A man wanting a wife in Switzerland stood on a mountaintop and hollered as loud as he could until one came running. Lord knows it was lonely on a mountain without a wife. It was cold, too. Even if it was just Piney Mountain and nothing quite as tall as Mount LeConte or ever so lofty as one of those mountains in Switzerland.

Foster went to a different church every week. Sometimes he rode further than the preacher did. He always washed up beforehand and wore clean clothes. He sang as closely to the right high notes and low notes as he knew how. He was polite and nodded to near everyone and smiled when it seemed appropriate. But he wasn't meeting anyone to be called on for a wife.

The protracted meeting at the little church outside Gatlinburg was one he'd sought out. A protracted meeting was like a revival, only longer sitting than that because it lasted one day. And it might take all day, from noon to midnight. More people came to church than usual when there was a protracted meeting, and Foster figured it was a better opportunity for meeting his future wife.

No one at the protracted meeting took a shine to him, it seemed. Maybe he'd have to wait until Easter and one of the mountain churches had an old-fashioned foot washing. Everybody came to that. Or maybe he'd meet a girl who didn't regularly go to church when they had a baptism shouting ceremony at one of the branch pools. Lots of people showed up for outdoor baptisms.

When the protracted meeting was over, the pretty girls left without asking Foster where he was from and what was his name. It was cold out.

He didn't blame them for running off to get warm. Foster said his goodbye to the preacher outside the church and stamped his feet to get them heated up. About all a sober man could do outside at night, if he was alone, was stamp his feet to stay warm. He pulled his wool cap on.

Foster kept a loaded pistol in a deerskin bag tied to his saddle when he was going to be on the mountain trails at night. Three or four times he'd heard a mountain panther scream on this side of Piney Mountain. It was the scariest thing you can hear at night in the mountains. It sounded like a woman screaming for help. Sometimes an old bear would be rummaging around at night, looking for trouble to get into. A bear had a noise it made that would have your horse stand up on its hind legs before you even knew it was hearing anything.

The preacher had talked a lot about hell that night, and the thought of it kept Foster warmer as he pushed his horse along the road at a canter. It was soon too dangerous for a hurried pace as the road became more like a trail and the terrain rose in uneven leaps of tree-covered rocky hill upon tree-covered rocky hill.

At one sharp turn, the sky opened between stands of trees. Someone had cleared land here. The moon shone. Foster saw a figure at the side of the widened trail. It was a woman.

He stopped before reaching her.

"Are you in need of help?" he called from horseback.

She didn't answer. She wore a dress with a light-colored apron. Foster let the horse walk. She didn't back away as he approached. Her eyes glowed like live coals.

"Howdy, ma'am," he said. "I'd be pleased to be of any assistance you might require."

Foster looked to the left of the woman, then over his shoulder. He leaned in the saddle and peered as far as he might in the darkness behind her. Couldn't see a thing. There wasn't a house. There wasn't a campfire. Nothing.

The woman held a stick in one hand, he saw. For fighting off bears, he thought, and panthers. Then he saw that she was barefoot. Had to be freezing her toes plumb off, he figured.

"Come on, get off the ground," he said. "I'll ride to where you're heading." He reached his arm down to her, and she took it. Sometimes mountain folk were too shy to talk to strangers, especially strangers of the opposing gender, but they weren't too shy to act. She hitched her skirt, then grabbed his arm with her right hand and let Foster pull her up onto his big roan.

When she was centered behind the saddle, she placed one arm around his middle. Her other hand kept hold of her stick.

"It's not far," she whispered.

She leaned against Foster as he urged his horse to a fast walk. He'd never felt anything so warm in his life. She smelled like lavender, he decided. And was as warm as coffee from the pot. He didn't have to worry about her being too cold. Maybe women were warmer than men all the way around, he considered. But the ones he knew always seemed just as cold as anyone else.

"My name is Foster. And I'd like to know yours, ma'am."

"Lucy," she said. She leaned up against him to say it, and he felt the word like heat on his neck. "I'm on my way home. It's not far from here. Just a ways, if you don't mind."

He didn't mind at all. Foster decided a warm girl like Lucy was the kind of woman he wanted to marry. He told her that he was a single man, that he owned a bit of land up the trail a piece, and asked if she was spoken for or no.

"No," she said. "I've got no one."

"You ever think of getting married?"

"Well, yes, I think about it," she said.

"I'll bet you do, Miss Lucy. I'll bet that's why you carry that stick, to beat back the boys with it. Boys must be always bothering a girl as sweet as you."

"No," she said. "I've got no one."

"Well, I guess you've got me," Foster said. He meant it in the nicest way. As a friend, if she wanted to think of it like that.

They'd only traveled about a mile's worth of mountain trail when she said it was here she wanted off.

"This is where I'm going," she said. Lucy slipped off the back of the horse.

"Wait," he said. Foster slid out of the saddle. His horse knew when to hold still. He held on with one hand to his horse's neck and pulled his boot off. He took off his green, wool sock, laid it over his shoulder, and pushed his foot right back into his boot. Then he did the other one. They were his Sunday socks and were in good order.

"You better put these on, you're going walking up that hollow." Foster held the socks out to her. "You can't go off into the woods barefoot. It's too cold."

"I can't take them," Lucy said. "I don't have anything to give you in return. I don't own a thing of my own."

Being poor was no crime. Besides, she owned plenty.

"You can give me a smile or a kiss, Miss Lucy. I'll leave it up to you. Either would pay me more than any ol' pair of socks is worth."

She took him up on it. Lucy pulled the socks on. She kissed him.

Her lips were like butter on hot biscuits. His heart heated up. He nearly fell over backwards.

Lucy turned and walked between two large trees. Must be a little cabin back in the woods, Foster thought. He memorized the spot and got back on his horse. In the distance he heard a dog begin to bark. Her home wasn't far. She was almost there already. Foster sang church hymns all the way home, his toes and fingers as warm as toast.

He told his mother the next morning that he'd met the girl he was going to marry. He told her that her name was Lucy. Foster said he owed it all to having attended the protracted meeting at the little church down Gatlinburg way.

"Did you meet her parents, Foster? Did they like you?"

"Well, no, I didn't."

"You had better ask them first before you plan to carry off their begotten. And there's someone else you ought to tell about this."

She was right. He ate his breakfast in a hurry.

"What color of hair does she have?" his mother asked, thinking of something. "Is she pretty?"

"I don't rightly know what color her hair is," Foster confessed. He headed out the back door. Oh, she was pretty. Foster was certain about it. A girl who could kiss like melting butter on a cold night was pretty as all get out.

His breath rose on the crisp morning air as he walked to the back of the hollow to share his news with the old Cherokee woman. Foster had a tin cup of coffee beans he'd scooped up from the kitchen table on his way out. You don't visit a neighbor without bringing something.

"Oh my Lord a'mighty!" the old woman bellowed when Foster told her about meeting Lucy. Her hands trembled, and her voice shook.

He stepped back. "What?" Foster said. Had he left something out?

"If you put that stick she carried into the mud it would grow a tree tomorrow," the old woman told him, clicking her tongue at the top of her mouth.

"No." He didn't believe her.

"Lord a'mighty, Foster, you grew up a stupid one when it comes to women, sure enough. That stick would grow a tree in one day, and that tree would grow poison fruit, and a white bird would come to live in it, and that bird would talk to you."

"A bird in a tree?" Foster was confused now.

"That bird would talk to you if you were dumb enough to listen."

"You think Lucy is a . . . a witch?" The old woman was just being mean. She was jealous that he'd found someone, and she was all alone.

"See there, Foster, you aren't as dumb now as when you walked in the door this morning. A witch is the least that woman is. Don't you dare be saying her name in front of me, not one more time, you hear! Lord a'mighty."

Foster left in a huff and a hurry. He knew the old folks said witches rode horses and cattle at night when they found a horse or cow worn out in the morning in a sweat with stickers in its tail. Maybe witches did bother the livestock when they had a mind to.

But Lucy was no witch. She hadn't scared his horse at all. She wasn't a witch just because she carried a stick. Foster must have told it wrong to the old Cherokee woman. He saddled his big roan horse before feeding her that morning and headed down the road from Piney Mountain till he came to the spot he'd memorized. It was the place where he'd dropped off Lucy last night.

He tethered his horse to a tree branch. The critter was hungry and might wander off to nibble on things. Foster walked off the trail, between the two big trees, following Lucy's route. He walked, and he walked. There wasn't anything back in there. A little spring gurgled over some rocks. A bit of ice glistened at the edge of the clear water, ice left over from last night. It would be gone if the sun got to it.

Foster climbed the rise behind the spring and looked high and low.

On a neighboring hill he saw a little tail of smoke lifting over the trees. He hiked to it. As he approached the clearing at the side of the hill, a dog started to bark.

The dog came at him like a beast from hell. In a dead run. Foster stood still as a tree. When the black dog got there, it stopped short and wagged its tail. It turned right around and led Foster to the yard in front of the cabin. Smoke poured out of the chimney on the end.

Foster hollered that he was coming to the door, but the dog's barking had amply announced his visit. The door opened, and there stood a white-haired man who, kicking at the dog to stay back, let Foster in. A white-haired woman removed a cast-iron kettle from beside the fireplace and poured Foster a cup of coffee without being asked. It was weed coffee, made from cooking plants from around the hills there, and not the real thing.

Foster sipped it and said his thanks. He told them where he lived and asked them if they were a big family or small.

"Just the two of us," the old man said. "We had us a child, but she died."

Sometimes the little ones did, Foster knew. And sometimes a woman couldn't have another one after that.

"I'm sorry to hear it," Foster said. Then he saw something hanging on a little nail by the fireplace. It was one of his Sunday socks, a long tube of green wool with the toe sewed across by his own mother. It looked damp and chewed on. "What's that?" Foster asked the old man, pointing at it.

"Something the dog brought home this morning. Carried it around the yard like he had a caught a rabbit on the run."

Foster thought about it. He was in the right neighborhood.

"You wouldn't know of girl named Lucy from around hereabouts, would you?"

The man gave him a strange look. His mouth puckered up, and his eyes glistened. The white-haired woman was behind Foster, but the young man heard her gasp.

"What?" Foster said. "What is it?"

"Well, that's our child's name. The one who died. She was only sixteen when the house caught fire. We lived about two miles over that way when the house was lightning struck and burnt down. We carried Lucy out before the house fell in. She slept up in the loft. But she breathed in too much of that fire first, and she died right away. Wasn't burnt any. Just breathed in too much heat. It killed her."

"I'm sure sorry to hear it," Foster said.

"We buried her a year ago yesterday," the old man said. "That's her dog out front."

Foster stood to go.

"I feel like I met your daughter," Foster finally said. He didn't say when. "I wonder if I did."

The white-haired woman was crying now. She sat in a chair in the corner and wept.

"That dog will show you her grave, you care to see it, son. We planted a laurel tree there with a line of rocks. It's over toward the main trail, by a spring. Our old place was up that hill."

"Thank you, kindly," Foster said. He got up and went outside. "Come on, boy," he said to the dog. And off they went.

Foster had already found the spring, he knew. The dog led him back the way he'd come. On the other side of the spring was a coffin hollow. That's a little sinking place in the ground where a person's been buried. You can see them plain as day you know what you're looking for. And there was a laurel planted at the head of it. It wasn't more than a stick.

That dog sat down and howled. It lifted the hair on Foster's neck to hear it do that. Then the dog jumped up and turned in circles, barking at its own tail.

"Stop it," Foster said. "Stop it."

The dog did stop barking. It stopped turning in circles. It stepped directly into the coffin hollow and started digging. It made fast work, and nothing Foster could say would get it to stop.

The dog quit on its own soon enough and came up with something that was buried there. It was Foster's other Sunday sock. The ground hadn't been disturbed in quite awhile before the dog started digging. Foster saw that was true. It couldn't have been that the dog buried his sock there the night before. Something else carried that sock into the grave.

The dog gave the sock to Foster. The long piece of green wool was warm from end to end. He shook the dirt off, and it stayed warm in his hands. Stayed warm like a kiss that would melt butter, like the breath of a fire.

Lucy wasn't a witch, after all. She was a ghost. She was a ghost you could kiss. Foster missed her sorely, though he'd known her only one night. He cried a little. He shooed the dog home and walked back to the trail, where his horse waited. Foster figured he'd be going back to church.

Private Places

*E*rica Johnson, at age eleven, woke up in the middle of summer to the worst day of her life. It was hard to believe things could be this bad when there wasn't school. But they were. She woke up without a piece of string around her toe. No string at all!

The oldest of six children, four of them brothers, Erica shared a trundle bed with her sister who was nine and a half. Their mother tied their big toes together the night before with a piece of string to see which one would marry first. The string was supposed to break in the middle of the night, and whichever girl had the shortest piece was sure to marry first and have as many children as she asked for.

Of course, if you woke up with no string at all it meant you would never marry. Somehow while they slept, her younger sister's big toe had stolen Erica's future right off her foot. It wasn't fair.

Erica was upset about it. She marched away from home to think it over. Her family's house was in the vicinity of the Dunlap coke ovens in the Sequatchie River valley. The long, narrow valley has sharply rising mountains on either side, the Cumberland Plateau on the west and Walden Ridge on the east. Top to bottom, the valley is one of the prettiest views in Tennessee.

The history of settlement in the valley is one of corn, cattle, and coal. The Sequatchie River valley was a fertile agricultural area. As well, coal was mined on Fredonia Mountain, overlooking the town of Dunlap.

The mined coal was brought down a 3,900-foot incline path to be processed in an area where more than 250 ovens had been built to cook the coal into coke, a concentrated form of coal that is used in foundries to cast iron and steel. The mine and the coke ovens were shut down permanently in 1927.

The beehive-shaped ovens, crafted by master masons of sandstone blocks, stood in long, staggered rows. Each oven was approximately six feet high. Railroad tracks were laid along the tops of the ovens so the mined coal could be delivered by train. Although more than seventy years have passed, many of the coke ovens remain, and the area has been turned into a park maintained by volunteers of the Sequatchie Valley Historical Association.

Though some were lost to scavengers and neglect, more than two hundred of the sandstone-and-brick ovens still stand, appearing much as they looked when first built between 1902 and 1916.

Erica had been warned against exploring any of the coke ovens or going too near any gopher holes she might find in the area. Gopher holes were long shafts mining companies bore into ground to test for ores. There were plenty of those in the area of Dunlap.

Before the park was built, the area of the abandoned coke ovens was eerie and desolate. Erica thought of the ovens as ancient ruins, long rows of dark mouths waiting to swallow little children. And bigger children, too. As Erica tramped through the area, she kept her mind on where she was going. She had the feeling that by passing the long rows of empty, black-mouthed ovens she was leaving modern-day civilization behind. Erica was on her own, slipping quietly into the past.

She soon came to a place where the trail split. To the left was the lane to the Orange Hill cemetery. She turned right. Erica was closing in on her destination. She passed by a big rock. The rock was where a night varmint stayed.

Erica had heard all about it. The varmint was supposed to have big eyes that shone brightly in the dark, but she had never seen it. She was not allowed away from the house at night.

Now on a ridge, Erica turned onto a trail that brought her about halfway down a long sloping hill. It was steep and beautifully wild along that trail. She came to the hidden road. It was mostly overgrown. If anyone used it, it had been long before Erica was born. It was just a little road you almost couldn't see.

She was halfway there. Erica followed the secret road for a mile and a half, even a little more, until she came to a stand of snowball bushes. They were the most beautiful snowball bushes in the world, and she thought of the stand of tall bushes as her own. Erica was the only person who knew they were there. The only one!

Later in life, remembering the snowball bushes in bloom would always bring her a moment's peace no matter what else might be going on. The snowball bushes marked her private place, the one place in the world where Erica could go to be safe and alone. It felt safe to her. And on that day, the worst day of her life when she woke up with no string at all tied around her big toe, she thought she was alone.

Just beyond the bushes was a flat grassy, mossy place. The trees around it grew stately and tall. The level area was good-sized, big enough for a cabin and a yard. It had grown up a bit, but it was still a beautiful place to sit and daydream in secret. Erica didn't know how she'd found it exactly. She just had.

Erica's shoe had come untied. That meant someone was talking about her, she knew. It was probably her sister asking their mother where Erica was.

She sat down on a nice flat rock and took off her shoe. A butterfly darted at her, then drifted away. She pulled off her sock, too. Erica studied her big toe. It was the culprit, the one keeping her from being married because it couldn't hold on to a piece of string tied around its middle.

Maybe there was something wrong with her big toe. It looked kind of funny. She bent it down. It didn't look too little, though, or too big for that matter. It might have been sort of short, she decided. And maybe just a tiny bit too straight.

Erica noticed a ladybug on her sock. She put her dog finger to it and let it climb on. Her father had told her it was her dog finger because it was a pointer. The red-orange beetle climbed the length of her finger like a ladder onto her hand. Erica lifted her hand to her mouth and blew on the bug. It flew off.

She recited the song she knew about ladybugs.

> *Ladybug, ladybug,*
> Fly away home.
> Your house is on fire
> *And the children are alone.*

That's when she heard it. That's when she heard something she'd never heard before. It was a sound so out of context that the eleven year old didn't believe she was actually hearing it. It was the sound of little children laughing.

Erica put her sock and shoe on. She searched the area. No one had followed her. No one else was there. When she stood still, she heard it again.

It sounded so much like children laughing that Erica had to struggle hard to believe otherwise, to convince herself that maybe what she heard was the sound of water babbling over rocks, the sound of water carried on the breeze. There was a spring nearby, and she quickly located it. It wasn't making any noise at all.

She stood perfectly still, pulled her hair behind her ear with one hand, and listened. The little children were laughing still. Then they spoke to Erica. They called out loud. Erica heard the words they spoke. "Hurry," a small voice said. "Come here."

There was no laughter now. The only sounds were those words carried by the small voices of little children. *Hurry. Come here.* And, *help.*

Eventually the words ended. There was no more laughter. There was the noise of a few birds chirping and the sound of Erica's own breathing.

She forgot all about never being married and walked home in quiet wonder. Erica went back the next day, and the sounds came again. First laughter. It was so close to her she thought she should be able to reach out and touch the children. Then the words. *Hurry. Come here. Help.*

Reluctant to reveal the existence of her secret place to anyone, particularly while the snowball bushes were in bloom, Erica did finally tell her mother. She had to know if other people ever heard voices in the woods, laughter on the wind. Erica didn't tell her mother everything, just that there were children laughing at a spot down the hill from the varmint rock.

Her mother said, if she had the place fixed right in her mind, that way back toward Upper Ten, a family once lived there. They had a cabin up high on a natural flat, but that the cabin had burned.

"Did they move away?" Erica asked.

Erica's mother told her daughter the truth. Two small children burned in the cabin. They were dead now. The family's name was Purley. The children's mother was out of the cabin, away but not very far. She rushed back when she smelled smoke and tried to carry water from the spring to put out the fire. She couldn't.

Her husband was off to the mines. The cabin burned down with the children inside.

"Their mother went in to try to save the children," Erica's mother said. "She went into that burning cabin twice and was burned severely. She never regained her sanity, they say, and she died in an asylum."

"That's just terrible," Erica said. She felt like crying.

"She'd been better off not to ever get married, I'd say," her mother said.

"You're teasing me!" Erica said.

Her mother smiled.

"Quit it, you hear." Erica caught her breath. She still felt like crying.

"The father moved somewhere else," her mother continued. "If it's the same place you mean, then that's the Purley place. Right where those big snowball bushes bloom."

Erica confided to her mother that she'd found a ladybug there.

While there are numerous public places of interest in eastern Tennessee, there are many private places as well. There are small, quiet spots to be discovered throughout the rugged rural areas—in the hollows and on rugged mountain ridges, by the waterfalls and deep in the forest-covered parks. The saddest ghost stories involve the ghosts of children. These stories occur in the smallest, most private place of all, a human heart met with loss.

Erica and her sister tied toes again one night in the fall. This time the string stayed on Erica's big toe. The piece of fuzzy yarn twine broke in the middle, which was more than good enough for Erica. She was going to be married after all.

A Cabin on Fire

Amos Milton Stevens had the habit of receiving inspiration for six-stanza poems while he was fast asleep in bed. The father of eastern Tennessee circuit preacher, J. Harold Stephens, Amos and his wife Eliza raised six children in a rural cabin tucked along the edge of the Cumberland Mountains. But it almost didn't happen that way.

Cabins catch fire.

The traditional mountain cabin, made of neatly dovetailed timbers, sported a roof that was covered with wood shingles split from two- to three-foot logs. A chimney stood at one end outside the house. The lower portion of the fireplace and chimney was often built of stones or local masonry. The upper third was commonly finished in a pattern of sticks plastered with mud. Mud was re-applied as needed.

A double-size cabin would have a chimney on both ends of the house. When a particularly hot fire sucked embers up the flue and scattered them across the wood shingles, a home caught fire from the roof down.

Because water had to be carried from a creek or spring, or hand-pumped from a capped well, and splashed onto a house a bucket at a time, mountain cabins rarely survived catching fire. Fire was a constant threat, even in warmer weather when a fire was stoked in the morning for cooking in the fireplace.

An early folk belief associated with the Appalachian Mountains holds that no amount of water will extinguish a fire caused by a lightning strike. Sweet milk is said by some to get the job done. Others report a preference for buttermilk.

Amos Stevens, the poet of his family, was aware of the risk of fire to a rural home and of the sudden and complete danger to life a house fire posed. But it wasn't the only thing he thought of when he went to bed at night. One midnight in early 1920, he went to bed and dreamed of possum. He woke up standing by the dresser and wrote out all the words to a twenty-line poem in honor of the American marsupial. He titled it *Ode to the O'Possum*.

The last stanza of the poem is remembered as follows:

> *You brag about your apple pies,*
> Of cakes both sweet and tall,
> But one little piece of possum meat
> *Most surely beats them all.*

Amos was inspired in sleep to pen verse. He wrote out the complete poem on his mind the minute he woke up. He wrote it out as if in a trance and read it as if he had never seen the words before when he woke in the morning. Some of his poems were short. Other times, they were quite long. In autumn, one came to him that was almost too long for his and his family's safety.

On November 11, 1920, Amos, the father of little ones, stood at the bedside dresser and wrote out the lines given to him in a dream. There were six stanzas of four lines each to this nocturnal masterpiece. The title was *Somebody's Cabin*. The words wouldn't mean anything to him until morning.

The first two stanzas were soon completed, and he scribbled away at the third, never wondering why he was writing the particular poem at hand.

> *The wind blows over the hill.*
> The sparks are flying 'round.

The cabin that stands by an open lane
Is rapidly burning down.

The strange thing about the situation is that his own house was thoroughly on fire while Amos was writing the poem. It's a true story. Amos Milton Stephens was a real man. And his house was really burning away as he scrawled out the four lines of the next stanza.

The owl is hooting back in the woods,
While sad hearts grope the ground.
The children stand in the field below
While the old cabin is burning down.

Actually, his children were still in the house. Fire climbed the walls. Amos penned his way through two more stanzas and laid his pencil down. He could have smelled the fire now. Somebody's cabin turned out to be his own. He woke his wife and rushed her and all the children, carrying blankets with them from their beds, to safety. Then Amos went back in for the family Bible he kept on the dresser by the bed.

He was burned, although not too severely, by entering the flaming home again. As did the cabin in his poem, the Stephens house burned to the ground. Amos had his family out, and he had the heirloom Bible in his blistered hand. Inside the Bible lay the folded sheet of paper upon which the words of his most recently completed poem had been written and saved. The fire claimed the remainder of his and his family's worldly possessions.

The complete poem and other works by Amos Milton Stephens were included in a long out-of-print memoir, *Echoes From the Hills*, self-published by the poet's son.

We do not know, nearly eighty years later, how Amos treated his blistered hands. It was rare that a doctor would be found for this purpose in rural mountain communities of the period. Certain mountain people in turn-of-the-century folklore were believed to have the power to talk fire out of a burn. Their treatment relieved the pain of a burn and aided in its healing. They were said to be able to blow out a burn as one might blow out a candle before going to bed.

Growly Apples

*A*ny place you find apples in East Tennessee you may be unlucky
enough to find a ghost as well. Everyone knows that the oldest apple tree
in a mountain hollow is haunted.

At the back rise of a cove up near the creek, or right down alongside
the road near the spot where a cabin once stood, the oldest apple tree is
the one you have to watch out for. Once the apples turn ripe and begin
to fall, you have to be especially careful to avoid a particular tree in eastern Tennessee that growls at anyone who stops to pick a piece of fruit.

People who've been scared away from the apple tree report that it
growls quite distinctly, frighteningly clear and loud. Those who've had
the misfortune to encounter it also note that the tree growls in a peculiar
manner. Not so much like that of a dog, it sounds more like a person
trying to talk, a person who can't.

Worse yet, if you carry off an apple or two from the tree, the apples
will growl when put away in the cupboard or a sack. They will growl
wherever you put them. Folks in East Tennessee call them growly apples
and wouldn't eat one on a dare. They know where the apples come from.

It was years and years ago at the end of October, about Halloween time, when Sud was showing off for the kids just before Sunday dinner. They had the preacher over.

Sud Eulitt was a handsome blond man with a pretty big mouth. He liked to make faces until whoever he made them at laughed. You had to laugh, or he'd never stop. He would make faces right through breakfast, Sunday School, and church.

The other thing Sud enjoyed was to eat apples whole. He did it just to show off. Said he learned from watching the horses eat. Sweet red apples were his favorites. He ate them, one big bite after another—seeds, core, stem, and all. Then Sud would smile real funny with his mouth crooked and his eyes looking off. Until you laughed.

One Sunday after church, while the preacher waited for the table to be set, Sud kept the kids entertained by making faces at them. Lisa and Lori laughed the most. They were sisters. If one laughed, the other one did. It didn't matter at what. Sud sat down at his own table, across from the preacher, and nodded to the clergyman without saying a word. They could smell the chicken in the oven in the kitchen.

Sud had a red apple in his hand. He leaned back in his chair, raised that apple to his chest, and stared like a goose right at the preacher. The preacher furrowed his brow a bit. Sud leaned back further in his chair and swung his arm in a wide circle at his side, like a windmill turning. He was winding up for the pitch, and the preacher was home plate.

All of sudden, Sud jumped up from his chair and flung his arm in a high overhand arch and stopped it halfway down as if to throw that apple right in the preacher's face. Sud was playing baseball. Lisa and Lori tittered. The preacher frowned, not taken with the game.

Instead of releasing the apple at the end of his pitch, Sud let the piece of fruit slip out of his hand backwards and bounce off his arm, almost straight up. Sud had practiced this more than once. He ducked his head back, looking straight up, and caught the apple as it came back down. He caught it in his mouth, which was big enough to catch an apple in.

Lisa and Lori clapped their hands with delight. The preacher shook his head slowly from side to side. What he didn't have to put up with to get some chicken and a piece of pie on Sunday after church. Sud bit the apple in half.

But he bit it a bit too soon. His head was still tilted back. The front half of the red apple plopped out of his mouth. Sud caught it in his left hand. He was supposed to.

The half of the apple inside his mouth lodged itself backwards, instead of ending up between his teeth where he could get a few more bites at it. It lodged way back in his throat. Sud couldn't even cough.

He made faces while his neck, and then his cheeks and forehead, turned red. Sud's eyes bulged as if they might pop out of his head. The children laughed. Sud stumbled back and forth across the room, knocking into chairs. Lisa and Lori laughed louder yet. Sud was a riot this Sunday.

By the time the preacher figured out Sud was choking it was almost too late. The preacher darted from the table, grabbed a good-size piece of firewood and ran at Sud. The preacher hit him square in the back with the firewood. Lisa screamed. Lori screeched like an owl. Sud dropped the apple half from his left hand, then fell to the floor on his side with a thud.

The apple didn't come loose from his throat, and his back was badly bruised. Sud lay airless on his side on the rug. Unable to breathe a lick, he turned slowly in place, kicking feebly a time or two with his feet. He quit turning red and turned blue—bright blue, then dark blue. His wife came in to see what the commotion was. The girls couldn't stop making noise. Sud was dead. People always said his big mouth would kill him. It did.

There was a spot in the yard Sud liked. It was where he would set his chair of a summer evening to smoke his pipe and watch the light go away when the sun went over the hill. They buried him at that spot. They put a marker up.

Sud's wife remarried and moved to another hollow with her two girls. She came back to visit Sud's spot a few years later, but the marker had been removed and there was a young apple tree in the spot.

The couple who lived there now said the marker got in the way of the tree, and they were real sorry to have to remove it. Sud's wife understood. Besides, she figured that apple tree was marker enough.

"It's growing right out of his head, I reckon," she said.

The couple nodded. It probably was.

Well, of course it was. They left that apple half in Sud's throat when they buried him. The roots of the young tree came right out of his eye sockets, and through his skull's big, wide mouth. One spring, the tree was covered with blossoms and bees. Later, it bore fruit.

The couple who moved in, along with their children, learned quickly that you couldn't pick the apples from the tree. Old Sud would let out an awful loud growl when they tried. And he wouldn't shut up. He'd growl away night and day until the couple brought the apples back, the ones they could, and left them on the ground at the bottom of the tree.

Birds ate at them, and a horse came by and ate a few. But soon the horse let out an awful whinny and ran off. The apples themselves learned how to growl. If you carried one away, a day or so later it would start grousing and moaning and growling like a man dying on the dining-room floor. That was the easy part to deal with, though.

What was difficult was when you ate one of the red apples from the tree that grew out of Sud's head. Your stomach would growl. And it would like to never stop. You couldn't go to sleep for a day or two and neither could anyone else close enough to hear.

When mountain cabins are abandoned, they fall in eventually. They are torn down sometimes. And sometimes they burn. Sud Eulitt's old cabin is gone now, but the apple tree is still there in an overgrown mountain hollow not far from the new highway. Tourists driving by sometimes see old apple trees from the road when they're in blossom or when they're bearing red fruit upon gnarled old branches bent low to the grass.

Tourists stop to pick an apple or two. It looks as if no one would mind. The trees aren't being pruned or well kept. There's a spring nearby in Sud's old hollow, and sometimes the visitors find it while they're stamping around the place. They almost never know a cabin was there. But when they get to Sud's tree, they hear about it. He starts growling right off. Most of them go away without picking an apple from the tree. The smart ones know a ghost when they come upon one.

Milk and Candy

*T*he frail woman was at the door again. And she was coming inside.

She came to Moody's store, located on the Childress Ferry Road, at the same time every evening. She showed up just as he was closing shop. She was barefoot and pale of skin. Her dress was gray with age and wear, its hem ragged. The woman's hair was undone. It was long and dark. It hung loosely down her back.

She carried a chipped china teacup in one hand. It looked like one someone had thrown away.

"Milk, sir," she said, setting the cup on the counter. She placed a thick reddish coin next to it. The woman never really looked at him. She never looked at anything but the hard candy pieces in the large jars he kept on the counter.

He filled her broken cup with milk, as much as it would hold. When he brought it back to her, she pointed at the piece of candy she wanted this time. She had done this every day for five days now.

"I have a nice piece of ham and a bone I could let you have," Moody offered. "There's a bit of cornmeal that's left over. I could give you that if you wanted. You could pay me at the end of summer, if you would like."

The frail woman was too skinny to be alive, he thought.

She shook her head at his offers and pointed at the piece of candy she wanted. Moody removed the jar lid and watched her slide her hand in to pick out one piece of candy. She never took two.

The woman left with her piece of candy and two ounces of milk. It was the same every time.

"You might as well face it," Moody's wife said. "She's a ghost."

"Her money's real enough," Moody argued.

They were strange coins, though. Large old reddish cents, like the ones from the colonial years. The surfaces of the coins were porous and a bit rough with age, but you could easily read the raised pictures on them. One was an Indian head. Another featured a horse's head and a plow. The words *Common Wealth* were spelled out in fat letters on the back of the latest coin she'd spent in his store.

"Pennies from off the eyes of the dead is what they are," Mrs. Moody warned her husband. "She's a ghost that's been robbing the graves next door to hers."

"All she wants is a piece of candy and a little milk," he said. Moody was becoming fond of his antique coin collection.

"No, dear husband. She wants much more than that."

"Why, the milk's for a kitten, I'll wager you. The lady has a pet cat. I'll give back every one of these coins, if she doesn't have a cat she's feeding."

Moody spoke with confidence, but he feared his wife might be on to something. He decided to follow the frail customer the next evening when she left his store. She always came at closing time anyway.

That evening she paid for her milk and piece of candy with a large copper coin that had the words *Nova Caesarea* in raised letters on one side. On the other side was a shield and the words *E Pluribus Unum*. It was good American money, after all. He put the coin in its place with the others.

Moody watched from the store window as the woman in the thin, gray dress walked along the length of his porch and down the wooden steps on the far end. She carried the cup of milk in front of her in one hand. She kept the piece of hard candy in her other hand in a fist held tightly at her side.

Moody went out the back door. He almost missed seeing her pass down the road. For being barefoot, the frail wisp of a woman walked swiftly along and was soon over the next hill. He had to run to keep up.

Moody followed her to Gunnings Cemetery.

His wife was right, he thought. He'd been taking money from a ghost. But wait! Maybe she was just walking through the burial plots as a short-cut to her cabin. Moody didn't want to, but he followed her into the cemetery.

Gunnings Cemetery is situated on a large hillside that slopes off into a wide cove, with steep, wooded hills rising alongside the other half. Moody watched the woman glide along in front of him to the back limits of the cemetery. The summer moon hung over the trees, but there was still daylight enough for him to see where she was going. She sunk right into the ground and disappeared.

He'd seen enough. Moody ran home. He told his wife. She told her two sisters. Someone told the sheriff. Someone else told Moody's brother. Before long, a crowd had gathered at the store.

"Don't eat another pickle unless you mean to pay for it," Moody told his brother. "We're running low."

"I can get you all the pickles you need," his brother said. "Susan put four dozen jars of 'em in brine."

"That, I did," Moody's sister-in-law said. "We'll bring a jar by Tuesday."

"Save them for your children," Moody said, giving in. "I don't suspect I'll run out of pickles that soon."

"We better look at the spot where she went down," the sheriff suggested. "If it's an unmarked grave, we better see what's what. I haven't been to no funerals for a month or more and the last one was old man John Topp's. Had a white beard growed down to his trousers, he did."

The sheriff brought a lantern. Moody and his brother carried shovels. The women huddled in a cluster of excited whispering as they walked the road to Gunnings Cemetery.

Moody showed them the exact place she disappeared. "She sunk right into the earth," he said. There was a mound of soft dirt encircled by grass. The mound had, in fact, been recently dug, perhaps within the week. Shoveling away the dirt was an easy task.

At the bottom of the grave they found a pine casket. It was a home-made pine box with a lid. Someone must have died up in the hills behind the cemetery. Someone had buried their own without a preached-over funeral. It wasn't unheard of. People caught sick and died quickly from time to time.

The sheriff held the lantern down into the grave while Moody and his brother pried the lid off the casket.

She was inside. It was the same frail woman that had been coming to Moody's store.

"For the love of God," Moody said. "It's her."

She looked more dead than usual. The shriveled corpse wore the thin, gray dress that was ragged at the hem. Her hair flowed down from her head in long dark tangles. Her eyes were closed in death, her mouth drawn tight against her teeth. The chipped teacup was at her side.

"May the Lord have mercy on her soul," the sheriff said. "Is that a sack she's holding in her arms?"

It wasn't a sack, exactly. The corpse held a newborn baby wrapped in swaddling. The baby was alive.

The women gasped upon the discovery.

"She's been getting the milk for the baby," Moody said.

Coffin babies were believed to have happened in history, when a mother died in delivery, before the baby was born. That was the likely case in this instance. The mother was buried, thoroughly dead, and sometime after the baby came into the world to find scant little room, no light, and only a tiny bit of air.

"It can't be alive," Susan said. "I don't believe it."

The baby was most certainly alive. It snuggled to its mother's chest, held tightly inside the dead woman's arms.

"Pull it free," Moody's brother said.

Moody tried. He couldn't manage it.

His brother set aside his shovel to help. One tugged at the baby. The other pulled on the corpse's arms. For all their labor, they couldn't free the infant child.

"She won't turn loose of it," the sheriff said. "But surely a mother wouldn't want her baby to die in the grave with her."

"She's worried for its well-being," Moody's sister-in-law supposed. "I'll give it a home. I'll adopt that baby as my own and raise it proper. What's one more to feed when you have six already? We'll adopt it, won't we, husband?"

Moody's brother agreed they would.

Upon hearing Susan's offer, the dead mother's arms fell away. The corpse released her hold on the baby.

"Praise God," the sheriff said.

Moody lifted the baby from the grave and handed it to Susan, who accepted it readily.

"Why look here," she said. "It has a piece of candy it's sucking on. Isn't that sweet?"

Moody and his brother put the pine lid back on the homemade coffin. They closed the grave, packing the dirt down good with their shovels. Susan sang a lullaby to her new baby. It didn't seem to mind hearing it.

The people present agreed to tell no one the origins of Susan's youngest, lest the baby grow up to be shunned. County records show a birth registered to Susan Moody that year. The gender of the child and its name are listed there.

Moody expected her back sometime, but the frail woman in gray never returned to his store. When he opened the box of antique pennies the woman had given him, he was surprised by what he found there. The coins were gone. And in their place were golden oak leaves, as many leaves as there had been copper coins. Moody had been bewitched by the woman's ghost.

He ran his store till he died an old man. Warrior's Path State Park is nearby. Park ranger and naturalist Marty Silver has located Moody's old store at the intersection of Old Mill Road and Childress Ferry Road. Although no longer in use, the building was still standing as this story was being prepared for publication. Gunnings Cemetery is still in use and is located near Exit 66 off Interstate 81 between Kingsport and Blountville.

Sweetwater Peach Pie

W hen Joshua Golden died, his widow took to making pies and wouldn't stop. Sally was already a good cook and a fine baker of fancy desserts. She got better at it. Peach pie became her specialty. She made peach pies summer, winter, spring, and fall.

Joshua had been well respected as a huntsman in the Sweetwater area of Monroe County. He hunted with a rifle his granddaddy had owned. It was a long rifle handmade by John Bull, of the type that made the Tennessee frontiersmen famous for their marksmanship. The rifle was loaded by placing a lead ball down the barrel, behind a charge of black powder, and ramming it tightly home with a rod before firing.

One day, Joshua was having a poor time of it. He rambled through the woods as far from his cabin as he had ever hunted before in a single day. He found nothing but squirrels. Joshua was after deer. Or maybe a wild turkey.

About when he was ready to head home, he slipped on a mossy boulder and tumbled down a steep ravine. He held onto his gun and kept the mud and leaves out of it quite nicely. But he couldn't keep from pulling on the trigger when he fell, and he fired a round straight up through the treetops.

Joshua didn't break any bones. He figured, though, that he had scared off any game on that side of the state. He dusted off his pants, pulled a thorn from the heel of his palm, and marched toward home. He'd get there about dark. He was getting too old for all-day hunts, Joshua thought. His legs ached and so did his hands.

Almost all the way home, just at the edge of his own property, right where you would never expect it to be, a young deer appeared in Joshua's path. It didn't smell the hunter and fed without raising its head. Joshua powdered his gun for the shot. Reaching for a ball of lead, he was shocked to discover he had none. The lead had dropped in the woods back where he'd taken his fall.

Joshua looked for a rock about the size of a bullet. There weren't any. The deer walked a few steps further down the path at the edge of the clearing.

Joshua was mad enough to spit. He thought he might pull one of his teeth and put that in his long rifle to fire at the deer. He wanted the deer that badly. But not badly enough to cut off one of his toes and use it for ammunition, he decided. Then he remembered the small, early season peaches he'd stuffed into the pockets of his hunting jacket.

He took one out and started eating it, as quickly and as quietly as he knew how, while tiptoeing along behind the deer to keep it in sight. Finally, Joshua was down to the peach pit. He sucked all the juice out of it he could, and forced the pit into the barrel of his gun. It took some doing and he made a little noise getting his ramrod down the barrel.

The deer stopped. It raised its head to see what the noise had been. At the same time, Joshua raised his gun and fired. He didn't give the deer a chance to run into the woods. Smoke poured out the barrel of his gun.

Joshua shot the deer. Not right where he aimed, but up high on the neck, just behind the ears. At least that was the story he told his wife. The deer ducked with the jolt of being hit. It staggered. Then it raised its head high, blinked at Joshua, and in tall, easy jumps disappeared into the trees.

Shooting the deer with a peach pit hadn't proved fatal.

"Where'd you get these little, hard peaches anyway?" he asked his wife a few minutes later, once he was home.

"A peddler come by with sacks of them on the back of a wagon," Sally said. "I traded eggs for them."

"Well, I hope you kept a couple back, cause that's what we're having for supper tonight. Those peaches aren't worth a darn when it comes to hunting with them."

After Joshua died, which wasn't long after that, Sally Golden remembered what he said. She was always looking for better peaches.

The Sweetwater valley has long boasted some of the state's prettiest farms. Peaches ripen here a little later in the season than do Georgia peaches and, because of this, some people think Tennessee peaches are sweeter. Sally knew for a fact that the peaches she got made better pies, better pies than anybody else's. She kept her peach source a secret from her neighbors.

Not long after Joshua died, Sally bought the woods that bordered her place. She put up *No Hunting* and *No Trespassing* signs. There were many good places to hunt nearby, so there were no trespassers. Folks figured that the widow didn't want people walking through the woods up to her backyard and stealing food from the garden, or running off with one of her chickens.

After eating a peach pie at a church social, the preacher told Sally she should enter her pie in the competition at the county fair. She did, and it won first prize. It earned for her a blue ribbon and fifty cents. Then all the desserts that won blue ribbons in their categories were judged against each other and Sally's peach pie won first prize again, earning a much fancier blue ribbon and another fifty cents.

Sally became famous for her peach pies. They won first-place ribbons in the all-around dessert competition every year at the county fair. There wasn't a whole bunch of frill to her peach pies. They were just good. Very good.

Other cooks became jealous. They thought she was using a secret ingredient that made her peach pie tastier than everyone else's. Ladies from her church were especially suspicious, because Sally could produce a freshly baked peach pie in any month you wanted one. Most people only had dried peaches out of season and dried peaches don't make the best pies. Sally's peach pies were always the best.

The opinion was that Sally had an extremely deep root cellar, or some place even deeper than that for storing peaches. There are some famous caves in the area of Sweetwater, Tennessee.

"Probably has her a hole into a deep cave in those woods back of her place," Nancy Card suggested to the other church ladies.

It was discovered that Sally bought more corn and more oats than a widow with no livestock of her own should be buying. Church ladies experimented with adding beaten oats and ground corn meal to their pie dough and fruit. It didn't help them any.

"I'll bet she's using maple sugar instead of regular," Nancy said. Maple sugar, commonly made in the area many years ago, was made by cooking down the winter sap of maple trees and then baking the resulting syrup until it was dry. The ladies found their own supply of maple sugar and tried using it in their pie dough and fruit. It didn't come out right.

"It has to be the peaches," Nancy told the others. "The Widow Golden doesn't have a single peach tree on her place. Not a one. I'll bet she's getting them from out of state." It wouldn't be proper to win first prize at the county fair using peaches from out of state. "Sally's pies ought to be disqualified to let someone have an honest chance at a blue ribbon," Nancy added.

Sally's peaches were just a little better than all the rest. Nancy and two others decided they were going to find out where Sally was getting her peaches. They asked high and low, from one end of the county to the other. Sally didn't get her peaches from any of the families in the area. None of the stores had sold peaches to her.

Nancy Card came up with a plan. After morning church that Sunday, she asked Sally if there was any chance at all she might be able to bake a peach pie for evening church, to give to the preacher as a special thank you, because it was the end of the month. Sally thought on it, then said she just might.

Nancy and her two friends followed Sally home. They hid behind trees and bushes and watched the front and back and side of her house. It wasn't long until Sally came out the back door with a metal pail in her hand. She'd changed into working clothes—plain dress and a clean apron.

Sally walked to the edge of the woods behind her house. Instead of picking peaches from a nearby tree, or digging them up from a hole in the ground, she spread out the contents of her bucket on the ground in front of an old stump. It looked like oats or maybe cornmeal.

Sally sat down on the stump and waited. She sang a song from church to herself.

Nancy's friends soon tired of watching her sit there. They had dinner to make for their families. They went home. Nancy Card stayed. She was determined to know what the Widow Golden was up to.

Sally sat on the stump and sang another song, and then another. Nancy leaned from one foot to the other, peeking from behind a tree. She was about ready to give up when she saw something strange. A tree moved in the woods behind Sally.

It wasn't a big tree. Nancy squinted. The tree was coming out of the woods. It was just moving along as pretty as you please. Nancy couldn't believe it. She held her hand to her mouth to keep from crying out. She closed her eyes tightly shut. When she opened them, the moving tree was still there, only closer.

Sally kept on singing. The tree stepped out of the woods.

Nancy could see it was a peach tree laden with fruit. There wasn't a lot of fruit, just enough for a pie or two.

The tree came right to Sally, and Nancy saw the truth of the situation. It wasn't a tree with roots. It was a tree growing out the top of a deer's head, where the antlers should be. It was quite a small tree, actually, but it was tall because it was atop a walking deer.

As the deer lowered its face to the ground to eat the feed that had been spread out for it, Sally gathered peaches from the tree and placed them in her pail. She patted the deer while it ate.

It was the animal Joshua Golden had shot with a peach pit before he died. The seed had lodged in the skin and grew a tree. The deer believed it had antlers like any other deer. Because the tree had a warm-blooded beast attached to it, it never froze. The little tree bore ripening fruit year round.

Nancy must have squeaked. When the deer was finished eating, it slipped back into the woods, the tree on its head disappearing into the other trees. Sally stood up and marched across her back yard, turning sharply just as she came alongside the tree where Nancy Card hid.

"Hello, Miss Nancy," Sally called.

Nancy stuck her head out.

"Would you like to come inside for a cup of tea, while I work on that pie you asked for? We could visit a spell."

"Don't believe I can today," Nancy said.

"Very well, then. Be seeing you at church." Sally turned to walk away, then stopped on a thought, and added, "I wouldn't be telling anyone about Joshua's deer."

"Oh, I wouldn't," Nancy said.

"I know you won't, dear." Sally smiled sweetly. "Why, the men in your family would have to send you off to the asylum were you to go around telling a story like that on a poor ol' widow woman. Now, are you sure you won't come inside and have an ogle at my blue ribbons? I put them on the wall in the kitchen, and they look quite nice there."

Snowy Footprints

*T*he cold winds blowing down from the Smoky Mountains in winter are as sharp as a barber's razor.

In the cabin on the west fork of the Little Pigeon River just south and east of Isaac Love's iron forge, a young mother huddled in bed with two of her children. Coffee boiled in a cast-iron kettle on the floor of the fireplace. Even though logs burned brightly nearby, it was warmer under the covers.

Wind came into the cabin from all four corners. And, every so often, someone threw open the door to come inside. Men and boys as young as fourteen warmed their hands and dried their feet by the fire before stamping off into the snowy fields to take part in the desperate search that was underway.

One of the woman's children had been missing nearly all day. Her husband was serving with the American armed forces in the trenches in France. The men in the search party didn't stay long. It would be dark soon enough. When night came, hope would lessen among the searchers that the woman's two-year-old son would be found alive.

The toddler had wandered off from the yard that morning, as the new snow and the temperature simultaneously fell.

She hadn't been able to find him, and he failed to answer her constant calls. The storm intensified. Her baby lost, she rode the family mule to a neighbor's cabin and asked for help. She barely made it back. Word was passed from cabin to cabin, homestead to homestead, church to church. By noon the search had begun.

The snow stopped briefly in the middle of the day, and the men were certain the little boy would soon be found.

He wasn't.

Dr. Thomas put on four pairs of socks and two pairs of trousers over his long underwear. He pulled on his great wool coat, scarves, hat, and gloves, and made his way to the cabin on foot. The doctor had come to tend to the lost boy's mother, but once there he realized the only remedy he could provide anyone was to help find the little boy.

He carried a lantern, as did some of the other men, knowing they wouldn't quit searching when night came if the little boy hadn't been found. A few of the men had their hounds. The doctor believed the dogs were far more likely to find rabbits than to find the missing child.

Dr. Thomas walked in a direction away from the river, into a large clearing from where, on a cloudless day, he could have seen big Mount LeConte and Clingman's Dome looking down at him. It was frighteningly quiet in the sloping, snowy field. The trees, he thought, were holding their breath as he walked by.

It began to snow again. The steep rise of white-blanketed hills surrounded him on three sides. Dr. Thomas climbed an unknown trail from ridge bottom to top. The work quickened and deepened his breathing. Time moved toward dark. The wind picked up, blowing snow. The evening was so cold it felt like swallowing bullets to gulp a mouthful of air.

He stopped time and time again, standing perfectly still to look in all directions for signs of life, for places a boy might be. There were many such places. Dr. Thomas trudged to each one to look more closely, to be sure.

At the opening of a long hollow shrouded with trees, Dr. Thomas saw something that looked like a footprint. Fox maybe. Or raccoon or dog. He bent over to study it. It was the footprint of a child, a barefoot child at that. There was another one and then three.

The snow fell thickly then, and the wind blew something fierce. He couldn't see a line of footprints in the snow when he looked up from the three he had discovered. There wasn't a trail to follow. Dr. Thomas was disappointed and perplexed. It was clear the boy stood here, that he had come this way.

Dr. Thomas turned a full circle, searching for anything, studying the snow at his feet, then studying the snow out in front of him a few inches and a few inches more. He found another one! He left his lantern there to mark the spot. It would be a place to bring more searchers to, if nothing else were found.

And then there was one more footprint yet. Oddly, the wind seemed to help. It was blowing the freshly fallen snow out of the footprints as Dr. Thomas slowly trudged along, praying for the next set of bare footprints to be revealed in the frozen snow.

His prayers were answered. The wind continued to blow the snow away and more footprints were revealed. They were easy to follow. The footprints brought Dr. Thomas to a clump of hemlocks, where the last tiny barefoot print of a toddler boy was blown clean by the wind. Dr. Thomas leaned forward and shook the snow from the lowest branches of a tree. He found the boy curled underneath the protecting arm of hemlock needles.

The boy was cold, though. He was not breathing. He was dead.

Dr. Thomas picked him up and placed the boy inside his wool coat, insides his plaid cotton shirt, too. If the boy couldn't have been warm before he died, he would at least rest in peace as warm as Dr. Thomas could possibly make him. Dreading what he would have to say to the boy's mother, he hiked back toward the cabin with his precious cargo, her deceased son.

At least, he had found the boy. By some miracle of wind and freezing snow on top of old snow, he had been able to follow the little boy's own bare footprints up the long sloping hollow to the hidden clump of trees.

He left his lantern at the place where he'd first seen the snowy footprints, in case she wanted to know where Dr. Thomas had found the boy. It was dark now, but the snow kept the night from being black. Dr. Thomas knew the way. It wasn't long before he topped the last hill. His feet were numb. So was his heart.

Dr. Thomas spotted the boy's mother on the front porch of her cabin.

She was wearing a blanket or a quilt. She was looking for something she didn't see. He could have hollered to her that he was coming, but he didn't want to. He watched her go back inside.

By the time he reached the garden fence that formed the border of her front yard, the boy's mother had opened the door again to look outside. She saw Dr. Thomas, saw that he was carrying a bundle against his chest. She called out her little boy's name and rushed to them.

"I'm sorry, ma'am," Dr. Thomas said. "I was lucky to find him, you see."

He unbuttoned his heavy coat.

She had her baby boy in her arms in no time, weeping with joy, trembling all over. She had every reason to be overwhelmed. The little boy opened his eyes and smiled to be home, to be in his mother's arms.

"Mom," he said in a small, weak voice. "Hold me, Mom."

Dr. Thomas was taken aback. But he carefully thought it through. The boy's vital systems must have been slowed from exposure to the severe cold. He hadn't died, but almost. The walk home with the boy against his chest, inside Dr. Thomas's clothes, had warmed him perfectly, slowly, until finally the tyke had roused as if from an afternoon nap in a sunny room.

"Thank you," the woman told him. "Thank you a mountain of gratitude from me and the Lord both. You come inside now and warm up. Why, you're a hero, Dr. Thomas, you saved my little boy."

"It was nothing," Dr. Thomas said. "I just followed his little footprints in the snow. The wind was blowing them clean for me. There was a line of barefoot prints in the snow right to him."

"Barefoot?" she asked, puzzled. "Did you say barefoot?"

She turned sideways, stepping into the light of her cabin, stepping inside. Dr. Thomas could see the little boy riding in her arms. He had on both his shoes.

"Show the doctor your shoes," she said to her son. He lifted his legs out from her.

Dr. Thomas saw that it was true. The boy had been wearing shoes the whole time.

"Been on his feet all day," she said. "Those are my knots. I tied his laces that way so he can't be losing his shoes down the well and such."

There were two other neighbors in the cabin. They patted Dr. Thomas on the back, and one of them handed him a cup of coffee.

"What's that about footprints?" one of the men asked Dr. Thomas.

"Oh, nothing. Nothing at all," Dr. Thomas said. He didn't care to talk about the barefoot prints in the snow to anyone just yet. "I thought the boy was already dead when I got there. Thought he might be dead all the way home."

"Mighty glad he weren't," the neighbor said.

Dr. Thomas woke up in his warm bed in the middle of that cold night with a clear mental picture of what had happened. Those tiny footprints in the snow weren't being blown clear of fresh snow as he followed along the path the boy took. Those little prints of bare feet in the snow had been made moment by moment, one after the other, as Dr. Thomas watched, as he followed.

He had been led to the boy, step by step, by either an angel child or a child's ghost. Dr. Thomas shivered with the thought.

Falling Down the Stairs

One of the very first homes in Cleveland, Tennessee, was built by the John McPherson family. The McPherson boys, a father and two sons, erected a sturdy, two-story log cabin soon after the town was created in 1836. The town and the McPherson family prospered. Cleveland became the Bradley County seat the next year. Before long, the McPhersons built a second two-story log cabin alongside the first.

There was a breezeway between the two buildings. This breezeway is referred to as a dogtrot by folks who study log-cabin design. But soon the breezeway was enclosed, and the roof was extended between the two structures, making one big house of the twin cabins. Other rooms were added over the years as McPhersons begot McPhersons.

All old, wooden structures make funny noises at night. The floor creaks, doors squeak, and the roof beams yawn in the wind. The folks who study log-cabin design don't have a name for it. No log cabin, however, has ever made the kinds of noises heard at night in the McPherson house. One spring in the 1890s, Allie heard the strange sounds when she came to the house to visit with her cousin Madelyn. The young girls' grandfather, Grandpa Mac, had died in the house the previous winter.

At first, Allie was more afraid of seeing the lady in the black shawl than she was of any noises she might hear at night.

"Grandma saw her," Madelyn told her cousin. The two girls were walking under the shade trees behind the house. "When you see her, someone in your family is going to die. She was right over there by the spring."

They walked toward the spring. Allie got chills thinking she might see the lady in the black shawl. She didn't want anyone in her family to die.

"Does the person who sees her ever die?"

"I don't think so," Madelyn said. "Just someone in the family will. Grandma saw her the day before Grandpa Mac died."

"What did she look like?" Allie didn't want to walk any closer to the spring, even though purple hyacinths were blooming there, and she wanted to put her nose to one and smell the perfume. It's what she best remembered about visiting her cousin the spring before.

"She was wearing a long blue dress. She always is, no matter who sees her. It's a long blue dress with big, soft pleats all the way to the ground. She carries a basket over one arm, and she's picking flowers, putting them in her basket."

Even in the dead of winter, the lady in the black shawl finds flowers to pick. She is never seen without her basket. No dog in Cleveland has been known to be brave enough to bark at the woman. Everybody knows dogs can sense a ghost.

"She will turn her face away from you if you try to look at her, and all you see is the black shawl," Madelyn told her cousin. "She keeps the black shawl up over her head, and you can't see her face."

Allie stopped walking. "I don't want to go to the spring today," she said.

And they didn't.

That night, after the supper dishes were washed, dried, and put away, Allie and Madelyn were taken to bed. Instead of a bedtime story, the girls told riddles with their grandmother. Allie's favorite that Madelyn told was *Round as a Cup*.

> *Round as a cup*
> *And deep as a cup,*
> *Yet the Tennessee River*
> *Can't fill it up.*

The answer is a tea strainer. The riddle Allie told that Madelyn couldn't remember the answer to was *Over the Hills*.

> *It goes over the hills*
> *And yells,*
> *But never eats.*
> *It goes to the creek,*
> *And hollers,*
> *But never drinks.*

The answer is a cowbell. Their grandmother liked that one.

"We should put a bell on each of you little girls, and see where you wander off to in your dreams at night," the older woman said. She kissed them each goodnight.

Late into that night's deep darkness, long after she'd been asleep, Allie heard an incredible noise. It wasn't cowbells, yells, or hollers. And she wasn't dreaming. The noise was real.

It was something awful. The noise was sudden and loud, and it woke her up. She was scared. It sounded as if chairs were tumbling around the house. Or as if someone was throwing them.

Madelyn, who was next to her cousin in the bed they shared, sat up, too. Allie was so afraid she couldn't scream. Madelyn put her hands over her ears and squeezed her eyes shut tight. The chairs kept tumbling.

Then they stopped, and there was one big *thwack!* It was a loud, hard thud. Allie thought the house shook just a little with the last sound.

Allie's mouth was wide open. She breathed as hard as if she'd been running.

Her cousin touched her gently with a reassuring hand and whispered, "Grandpa Mac. It's grandpa falling down the stairs."

Allie didn't say a word.

"He does it almost every night."

That's how their grandfather had died. It was a fact. He slipped in the middle of the night at the top of the stairs and fell all the way to the bottom. He broke his neck.

"Grandma says people born on Old Christmas don't completely die," Madelyn told her cousin. "She said a person's spirit keeps right on doing whatever it was doing when he died. So grandpa falls down the stairs about every night. Nothing else happens."

"Was he born on Old Christmas?" Allie asked.

"I suppose. When is it, anyway?"

"In January," Allie said. "Twelve days after the real Christmas."

The next morning Allie asked her grandmother if she, too, had heard the noise last night.

"About every night he falls down those stairs," the old lady said. "Been meaning to do something about it. I think he does it louder on purpose. Seems like he does it louder every time."

Allie bet it hurt to keep breaking your neck night after night. She felt sorry for her grandfather, and she was particularly happy her birthday wasn't in January, even if she did have to wait almost all year to get any birthday cards or presents.

"Maybe you should take the stairs out," Allie said.

Madelyn laughed. They couldn't do that.

But grandma didn't laugh. She looked right at Allie and sort of smiled at the little girl. "Maybe," the old lady said. "Maybe we could do just that."

Since the house had been two two-story cabins to begin with, there were two sets of stairs. One on the left side and one on the right. The girls' grandmother had some men come by that day after their work. The men took the stairs out.

They also sealed the room off at the top of the stairs. They boarded it up. Grandpa Mac's ghost had his room all to himself now. He couldn't get out. The stairs he had fallen down were gone. He wouldn't be able to hurt himself.

Allie couldn't wait until her mom and dad came to pick her up at the end of her two-week's stay-over. She would show them where the stairs were gone and tell them that it was her idea and grandma had it done. Just like that. And now Grandpa Mac's ghost wasn't falling down the stairs every night and breaking his neck. And now the noise wouldn't wake anyone up. The noise wouldn't bother anyone ever again.

Well, almost.

That night both Allie and Madelyn were again rudely awakened by a sudden noise in the house. They sat up in bed and blinked their widening eyes in mostly wonder, and a little bit of fear, upon hearing a loud, solid bump. Like someone kicking a door. While their eyes were still adjusting to being open in the dark, the second sound came. It was the same old *thwack* they'd heard before.

Grandpa Mac had kicked open his bedroom door, they figured, and fell like before. Only there was just one big bump at the end of his fall because he didn't have the stairs to tumble down anymore. The two little girls went back to sleep. Some nights the sound of their grandfather's falling and breaking his neck didn't even wake them up.

The McPherson house has survived the War Between the States, two world wars, and was still standing in the 1970s when Grandpa Mac's story was first told to non-family members. The shade tree is gone. The spring has been capped off. But the lady in the black shawl is spotted today from time to time by the townsfolk, as she picks flowers or herbs along the railroad tracks. She's a community legend now. No one has yet seen her face. No one much wants to.

Parked in front of the sprawling, two-story log house, originally built by the McPhersons in the 1830s, you are likely to find a pair of newer model cars. The house has been treated to a clapboard veneer. The yard is green most of the year and fastidiously kept. A few hyacinths bloom each spring, the first of the perfume flowers to announce the change of seasons with their heady scent.

Inside the carefully tended house, the ghost of an old man still stubbornly falls to his death once every night. Grandpa Mac tumbles nightly down a set of stairs that is no longer there and, whether or not he was born on Old Christmas, has become the thing that goes bump in the middle of the night in Cleveland, Tennessee. Sometimes, it will barely wake you up.